READY TO BLOOM

Book Two of The Curvy Lane Series

SARAH GAI

CHAPTER ONE

*S*avannah

"CAN I get everyone's attention please?"

I clinked a fork against my champagne flute before placing it back on the table. When everyone at the engagement party quieted down to listen, I turned to the beautiful couple standing beside me.

"I just wanted to give a quick toast to Alyssa and Flynn to let them know just how happy I am about their upcoming wedding. Now, I don't want to say too much, or else I'll have nothing funny to add for my wedding speech," people laughed and of course I took pause, "but let's just raise our glasses to the happy couple and congratulate them!"

Alyssa stepped out from Flynn's hold as everyone cheered and wrapped her arms around me. "You're seriously the bestest-estedest friend any one could ask for, Sav."

"Yeah I know," I pulled back and smiled at her.

Moments later many of the party goers came up to talk to the couple and I removed myself out of the fray. I loved people, but I dealt with people on a daily basis, and even though I enjoyed a crowd from time to time, that night all I felt was a stupid kind of melancholy about the situation. I walked down from the patio and towards the seating by the pool. Mr. Colson's property was beautiful and always manicured. It was so sweet of him to host the celebratory event for his son. I guess it was his proud moment.

As I sat down on one of the cushioned wicker chairs, I looked back up at the back deck and spotted Mr. Colson laughing and talking with Alyssa's mother, Teresa. I could tell that was one pair of in-laws who were going to have no trouble getting along.

As my eyes moved from them, they landed on my other best friend Willow. The moment she spotted me, I managed to give her a smile that obviously didn't meet my eyes, which she had picked up on because within a few seconds she was off the porch and speedily walking towards me.

"Hey chick, everything okay?" she asked as she crouched down in front of me, pulling the champagne flute from my hand and drinking it.

"Ah, I was drinking that!" I crossed my arms.

"No, you were swirling it. How do I know? Because it was warm. Now tell your friend Will what's wrong."

"Nothing's wrong. Just tired I guess."

Willow stood up and towered over me. "I call bull. Come on, last chance before I walk away."

Leaning back in the chair, I sighed. "It really is silly. I remember me and Chris talking about getting married one day. I thought I would be the first of us to tie the knot I guess, and well, here I am, years later still single, still alone, and I can't see that changing anytime soon." Willow crouched again and placed her hands on my knees. "Sav, I know you don't want to hear this because you still have feelings for Chris, but I promise you will have your own engagement one day, to a man who won't leave every time someone else comes along."

Ouch that hurt! I reached up to rub at my chest.

"You're going to find a man who thinks the sun shines just for you, and that man will love you for you, okay?"

I nodded, and couldn't help but smile at my dear friend. She wasn't the gooey feelings type, so to remind me I would one day move on and find my very own Mr. Right was kind of sweet. Will stood up and placed her hands on her hips. "So, we all good here, or do I need to take you home?"

I held out my hand and she took it to pull me up. I hugged her. "Nope we're all good and I feel a lot better, thank you."

She let go and stepped back. "Ah all in a day's work for this lady. Now, I'm going to grab a drink and check out all the single tradesmen. Have you seen some of the guys Hudson and Garth work with?" She gave me two thumbs up as she backed away towards the patio.

I couldn't help but laugh at my man-crazy friend as I turned and decided to check out the rest of the back garden. Leaving the pool area, I walked onto the large expanse of grass. String lights were hung, illuminating the large oak trees. Just below were several tables with trays filled with meats, cheeses, breads, and dips. Willow and Hudson had done all of the food prep while I arranged the floral centerpieces. And of course one special table was set up with candy from Alyssa's new venture, Just as Sweet Candy Buffet, the new extension of her business. I even loved how at her own engagement party she had business cards on display. I picked one up and held it in my hand marveling at the beautiful display. Seeing my friend happy was what mattered most.

"So I happen to know the young lady that owns this candy buffet. I could get you a discount for your next event if you're interested."

I had come to know that deep husky voice well, and it lit me up in ways that had my body warming. "Hey, Hudson," I turned to look at him as he came up beside me. Had to creak my neck a bit because he was at least a head taller than me, and at 5'7" I wasn't short by any means.

"Are you enjoying the night.?" he asked.

I didn't know why, but I got the impression that sometimes Hudson was a little nervous around me.

Then again, I wasn't an expert on men and body language apparently.

"Sure am," I lied. What I really wanted to do was get back to my empty house and bead some bracelets. I know weird, right? But that's what I did when I was sad or upset, anxious or unsettled. Made me feel better.

"So… any plans for the rest of the weekend?"

"Yeah, tomorrow Willow and I are going to a trade show. She makes her own coffee beans now, so we want to put them out there for suppliers to try to draw awareness to it, I guess. So yeah, I said I would help."

Hudson nodded and then scratched at his perfectly trimmed beard. It was cute. I didn't know why, but it was. "Shame. Garth and I are heading out fishing tomorrow and I thought… oh well, never mind. Anyway, enjoy the rest of your night."

"Yeah, you too," I replied and Hudson nodded at me before taking his leave. However, I wasn't sure I wanted him to walk away. I enjoyed his company, I just wished he would ease up around me a little more. After all, we were friends.

I FINALLY MADE it home to my empty house and settled in on the sofa. I immediately put the Hallmark Channel on the television for the noise so the place didn't feel so lonely. Next, I grabbed my craft supplies and scattered them in front of me on the coffee table and started sorting through beads. Alyssa spent most of her time staying over at Flynn's in the bungalow, and though I was really happy for them, having a quiet house reminded me of just how alone I was. Soon enough, I would have to talk with her about whether we were going to sell the house, or if I should think about getting a roommate to help pay the mortgage and… keep me company.

Finishing my beaded bracelets, I placed them in the large resealable bag filled with all the other pieces I had worked on the past few weeks. I did so many of them, I wound up donating them to thrift stores. Alyssa and Willow thought I was mad and what I really should have been doing was selling them in my flower shop. But for me, I liked giving them away. At the same time, it could bring in extra revenue, and as of late, I had seriously started thinking about just testing a few pieces out and seeing if customers would be interested.

My phone buzzed and I looked down at the sofa cushion beside me. It was a message from Hudson. Picking it up, I swiped at the screen and read the message.

Home safe?

He really was sweet, and not just because he texted me but because he was so considerate. For the past year he had been buying flowers from me for his grandmother every week. I didn't know too many grandsons that were as doting as Hudson.

I'm safe & sound and ready for bed.

Hudson was always looking out for me, too. I

considered him a friend, which was a good thing seeing as we were around each other quite a bit these days.

Sleep tight and hopefully I will see you next week sometime...

I sent him back a thumbs up emoji before getting up off the sofa and padding towards my room. Snuggling down deep and comfy beneath my comforter, I reached for the remote and switched on the television sitting on top of my dresser, needing the low volume noise to help me sleep.

Oh, but fate was being cruel in that moment, as the first thing that came on was the car dealer ad... with my ex's face plastered on the screen in front of me, looking all kinds of handsome. The beautiful jaw line, the smoky eyes, dark hair, and a smile that floored you... he could have been Elvis's son or at least a descendant of him. *God, just what I wanted to see.* The stark reminder I wasn't good enough for him. Yeah, life could definitely suck...

CHAPTER TWO

$\mathcal{H}$udson

"Man, last night's party was killer! And did you see Willow? Knockout kind of beautiful! Oh and the game she's playing, trying to act like she doesn't notice me."

I shook my head at my friend because for one, he was scaring the fish away with all his talking, and two because he was clueless. "Garth, I don't think that's a game."

He scoffed. "Trust me, she sees me, and she definitely knows I see her."

"Of course she does, you're not exactly stealth about it." Garth placed his fishing pole in the metal holder he had pushed into the ground and turned to face me with his hands on his hips.

"What's got you in knots today? You've been pretty short with the way you're talking to me."

"Nothing. I just want to fish and enjoy the quiet."

"Liar!"

I didn't respond. But my friend was right. I had become frustrated of late. My brother fell in love and got married to the woman of his dreams while I was still single at thirty and had spent the past year chasing someone who didn't even realize I was chasing her.

God, the moment I laid eyes on Savannah at Haggart's Market just over a year ago while shopping for my weekly fresh vegetables was like bam! Bam! Bam! She went straight to my heart. I needed to know her, I had to. This beautiful auburn-haired stranger with curves that begged me to touch them and amber green eyes that smiled when she spoke was like a siren calling me with her song and my feet carried me towards her store without a way to stop myself. Yeah, I was a goner the moment I spotted her standing behind the counter of her flower shop. So every Saturday since that first sighting, I went to the market because I knew she would be there, and every week I bought flowers for my grandmother, who had passed away, just because I needed an excuse to say hi. But Savannah didn't know about my grandmother.

But besides that, who was I kidding? I bought the flowers for myself, and every time I looked at the arrangement throughout the week, I thought of that curvaceous woman. Shortly after, my co-workers started wondering why I went to the market every week. Nathan, one of my employees, and my friend Garth, who named the strip of stores that held the girls shops Curvy Lane, occasionally tagged along. They were not wrong because it was like walking into a Christmas dream every time. The smell of freshly roasted coffee and delectable cupcakes from Bit of Spice lead to the colorful array of candy from Just as Sweet, and then the fragrance and spectacular arrangements of flowers from Ready to Bloom should have been enough, but in every store was a curvy beauty with smiles that could light up the night sky. It was my favorite aisle in the entire marketplace, and one that had me returning every damn week.

"Dude, you just need to ask her out." Garth pointed out.

I scoffed and reeled my line in to rebait. "I'm pretty sure she would turn me down."

"Why? You're a handsome man. You've got strong arms, you're as tall as a tree, and that beard is in fashion now. I mean, ladies love that whole logger look. Heck, you even wear the flannel shirts," he said and winked my way.

"I don't know whether you are complimenting me or hitting on me. If it's the first, thanks, I guess. If it's the second… thanks again, I guess. It's nice to be noticed."

"You're welcome. But Hudson, I'm telling you, if you want Savannah to notice you, then you gotta pull yourself out of the friend zone box she has placed you in and just make your intentions known."

I recast my line back into the river and sat down on the camp chair. "I don't know how to do that."

"Come on. There's gotta be something. I mean… for example, she and Alyssa bought a fixer upper. You work in the building industry." He wiggled his brows.

Oh he was good. "You're right. I'm just a guy who wants to help."

"Yes, you are."

Damn, my friend was good. I might rip on him every once in a while with his bold personality and lack of filter. But on the occasion, he had some pretty good ideas. This one about helping her fix up the old house in need of some serious TLC was the perfect in—and an opportunity I wasn't about to waste.

CHAPTER THREE

*S*avannah

"So, what have you ladies got planned for tonight?" I asked my two friends as I stepped into Alyssa's store, also known as our mid-meeting point. My store was on one side and Willow's on the other.

"Flynn and I are actually going out to taste test cakes for the wedding." She sighed and, once again like I had been witnessing for months, hearts popped out her eyeballs. Okay, not literally of course, but the way she was daydreaming and gushing over her man, well, it was enviable.

"Oh okay, so are you coming back to the house tonight?" I threw it out there.

Alyssa paused what she was doing. "Savannah, is everything okay?"

I shrugged my shoulders, "Yeah I just miss you is all. It's really quiet without you most nights, and so I wind up putting on the Hallmark Channel cause it makes me feel like you're there."

She walked around the counter and hugged me to her chest. "Well, then how about we have a girls night this Friday, hey?" I pulled away and waved her off. "You don't have to do that for me."

"Are you kidding? Flynn's a grown ass man, he'll be fine by himself. Besides, I love girls night."

"Count me in," Willow called before she walked away from the coffee machine, leaving Alyssa and I alone.

As I was about to turn and head back to my shop, I paused and swiveled around to face my friend once again. "Alyssa, can I just ask you a question before I go?" I figured now was as good as any other time to sort out the housing issues.

"Sure what is it?"

"Okay, so no matter what you say, I'm totally happy for you. Um, I know in a few months it's going to be official and you'll be moving in with Flynn, so… are we going to have to sell the house?" I don't know why I cringed in that moment but I regretted even asking.

She smiled at me. "No, we're not going to sell the house."

I felt the relief of not having to find another place and relaxed my shoulders. There was this kind of a heavy moment that fell between us, as if this talk was the realization for Alyssa that life was about to change in a big way.

She took a deep breath and clutched at her stomach. "Wow, I can't believe we're talking about this… I wasn't expecting it. I mean, I knew things would change, but I just hadn't really processed it with all the engagement and wedding planning. I'm… moving out, and I won't be living with my best friend anymore."

"Do you think I should start looking for a roommate?"

"Is that what you want?"

I shook my head and smiled playfully. "No, I want you, and only you!" She laughed and then the heaviness dissipated.

"What about Willow?" Alyssa suggested. "I mean, she lives alone and she's just renting a duplex right now. Maybe you could be roomies."

I held out my hands in a hold-on-one-minute-missy kind of way. "Oh nope, no way. I love her, like a lot, and she's one of my best friends and all, but she's… loud, if you know what I mean."

"I heard that!" she called from her shop and I turned to meet her glare as she stood once again at the coffee machine.

"Well, it's true and I don't want random men coming and going from my house."

"Well, not that I'm moving in with you, but that wouldn't happen anyway because I always go back to their house." She turned and walked away with her nose in the air.

"Anyway, let's talk about this roommate situation later because…" Alyssa drew out her sentence as she looked past me and waved, "Hudson is here."

I turned my head to look at him. *Gah!* The man was cute that was for sure. I hated to admit it but every time I saw him, those first few seconds always caused my heart to stutter and my legs to go a little wonky. There was no denying the fact I found him attractive. You would have to be blind to not be affected by his very presence. And if his looks didn't cause you to drool, his gentle nature, kind words, and caring ways would steal your heart anyway. Oh, and when he spoke… the gruffness in his voice mixed with the lowness of his vocals… he was face fan worthy.

But he wasn't keen on me that way. At first, I thought he was coming around because he may have been interested. I even thought if he had asked me out in the beginning I would have said yes. But months went by and he never approached the topic. Truthfully, it was probably a good thing because I wasn't over my ex. I'm still not over him in a lot of ways and that was something I was working on every day.

As for Hudson, I just settled with the idea that he just saw me as a friend, and I was okay with that. Even if he did stir up those pesky butterflies in my stomach. Not to mention, soon he was going to be my best friend's brother-in-law, which meant I would be seeing him more and more, so somehow I was going to have to learn to control my inner blush around him.

"Hey, ladies, fancy running into you all here," he joked as he entered the store.

Alyssa leaned across the counter and Hudson brought his face down to meet her as she kissed his cheek. "What brings you here? You never do your shopping until Saturdays, and it's only Wednesday."

"Actually, I'm here to talk to you and," he pointed at me, "to you."

$\mathcal{H}$udson

"Oh, okay is it anything important?" Alyssa asked as she leaned on the counter, a look of worry on her face.

"Yeah, it kind of is," I replied.

I should have kept my focus on Alyssa, I knew better than to look at Savannah head on when she was so close. But I couldn't help myself! One glance was all it took and her eyes held me captive. God, she looked beautiful. The weather was heating up as we had just walked into the summer season, so she was wearing a pastel green floral ankle length dress, her auburn hair hanging just below her shoulder. And those lips painted pink and shiny… I could stare at those lips all day.

"So, what's so important?" Alyssa snapped her fingers to get my attention.

I shook my head and with every bit of strength I had I managed to turn my head back to face my future sister-in-law. "Right, your house is falling apart, gutters are coming down, walls need fixing, so Flynn, Garth, and I are coming over this weekend to fix it up."

"Hmm, Flynn didn't say anything to me about it."

"That's because he doesn't know yet."

"Okay, so what brought this on?" Alyssa asked, eyeing me suspiciously and tapping her nails against the glass countertop.

"I just… thought it was a good idea. Actually, it was Garth who mentioned it."

"Oh, you don't have to do that. I'm sure we'll get around to hiring someone." Savannah waved off my offer.

"Why do that when you know a bunch of trades-men?" I replied, glancing her way.

Savannah shook her head. "No really. We can't ask you to give up your weekends doing what is our responsibility."

"Actually, I think that's a great idea," Alyssa spoke up excitedly. Oh she was good, giving me the briefest of nods, catching on to my plan. "And if you have time I'm sure you could drop over throughout the week if you knock off early to finish some stuff"

"I could," I replied, falling more and more in love with the notion that she would soon be my family.

"And even if I'm not there, I'm sure Savannah could rustle you up some dinner."

"Yep, it's called take out because I'm the world's

worst cook," she laughed. "Oh, a customer! Later!" She waved as she rushed away and then stopped to look back. "Are you coming here Saturday or do you want me to just bring your grandmother's flower bouquet home with me, seeing you're going to be there?"

"Home is fine."

"Okay," she said before she ran off.

"Yeah, Hudson, it's so sweet of you to still be buying your grandmother flowers seeing as she's dead!"

I turned to look at Alyssa standing with her arms folded and an amused look on her face. I rubbed at my neck. "It's the only thing I could come up with at the time, and well, after a while I couldn't tell her I lied. Besides, I like the flowers."

"Well you need to tell her sooner rather than later."

"I'm working on it, Lyss."

"Nice idea about fixing up the house though. Make sure you utilize it and get out of the friend zone, mister," she pointed a finger my way.

"Oh I'm working on that too. And how did I even get in there?"

"Because you're sweet and you don't have a pushy bone in your body, not like that brother of yours. But Hudson, a word of advice, she needs to be pushed. No, it's more than that, she needs to see you're interested."

"Noted. Let her know without a doubt I'm interested."

"That's right, easy peasy," she giggled.

I stayed around for a short time as Alyssa explained all the things she still had to do for the wedding. "And don't forget, no strippers, Hudson. I mean it." She pointed at me again and I couldn't help but roll my eyes, and I wasn't even an eye roller.

"I know, jeez woman you've told me like twenty times already."

"Okay, I'm just making sure. You're the best man so you need to be responsible."

"Once again, noted. Okay, so I'm going to take off. Is it possible for you to get me a spare key to your house so I can go get an idea about what I need for Saturday?"

Alyssa crouched down behind the counter as I waited and popped back into sight a few seconds later, twisting a key off her chain. "Here, you can have mine. I'll get another one cut later," she handed it over to me.

Thanking her, I left Haggart's Markets and drove straight to Savannah's house. I had been there a few times before, but never for long. My father's house always seemed to be the place for everyone to catch up. It helped that me and my brother still lived there. He roomed in the pool house, but I was still in my childhood bedroom. Didn't bother me that I still lived there, even when the guys at work heckled me for it. We all had our space, but since my mother passed away a few years back, I just felt my father needed us there. Maybe not so much these days, but still, I was happy. And who wanted to go home to an empty house every night?

As I inspected what was needed to fix Sav's house, I wondered how she was going to feel once Alyssa left. She didn't strike me as someone who enjoyed her own company. For the briefest of moments, I thought about the prospect of moving in with her, and then quickly threw that thought to the curb. I wanted her to know I was interested in her, not scare her off by suggesting I be her new roommate.

Yeah, she would be the only reason I would move out. But, I had to play it smart, and truthfully, I wasn't as bold as my brother Flynn. When he saw Alyssa for the first time, he just went for it. I wish I had half his confidence when it came to the opposite sex. Sure, I had rustled up the nerves to ask some women out before, and some of them had turned into a second or third date, but I had never felt an inkling of adoration the way I felt for Savannah, and that kind of terrified me.

As I locked the front door, happy with what supplies, tools, and materials I would need for the weekend, I got into my truck and headed for the hardware store. I don't know how many times I rehearsed the simple line "Will you go on a date with me?" in my head. Somewhere in my mind I thought by repeating it to myself I would suddenly find my boldness.

Yeah, I was so out of my depth. But I had to get out of the friend zone box and make her see me as more.

CHAPTER FIVE

$\mathcal{S}$avannah

I CLOSED up the shop a little earlier than I usually would. Saturday trade was a good day for me and I knew I would be losing those extra dollars I desperately needed, but I was a little excited to see what the boys had achieved.

When we bought the house at an auction three years ago, Alyssa and I knew it needed a lot of work. And we were all gung-ho on doing it, too, but we had no idea what we were doing or the amount of money it would take to complete the renovation, so it kind of took a backseat.

I waved goodbye to Willow as I walked past her store, not even having the courage to glance into Just as Sweet. With Alyssa's candy buffet business growing, she worked most Saturdays and Sundays doing private parties. It was good for her and bad for me because as of next week her Sunday employee Amy was going to be working five days a week! She was nice and all, but I would miss Alyssa so much, and my days wouldn't be the same not seeing her there or being able to talk to her whenever I wanted.

Pulling up to the house, I parked along the sidewalk since two trucks were loaded and parked in my driveway. I reached for the bags and the bouquet on my passenger seat before exiting my car. The front lawn was littered with planks of wood, paint cans, and equipment I tried gracefully to weave between. I didn't see the tool box until my foot hit it and I went for a dive head first over it. The thing I learned was when you're in the middle of a fall, just go with it. Don't flail your arms and try to fight to stay upwards, as it just makes the ultimate decline that much longer.

"Crap, are you okay?" Garth asked as he helped me up, grabbing me under both arms and pulling me back up to stand.

"Yeah, just clumsy and didn't see it," I replied as I looked down at my muddy and grass-stained white tank. At least the take-out bags were still on my wrists, but the flowers were scattered near the front door.

Garth ran to pick them up and as he handed them to me, he looked past me. "Willow not with you?"

"No, why would she be? She's still at the shop."

He shrugged "I don't know, just thought you being besties and all, she would be here with you."

I grabbed his cheek and then patted it. "You're so adorable. You just keep trying to catch her, Garth."

"Oh, I will," he winked.

"So what are you doing out here by yourself?"

"I'm replacing some the weatherboards that are rotten."

I cringed. "How bad is it?"

"Well, apart from the gutters and some wood rot, the outside is all okay. We really just need to sand it and give this baby a fresh coat of paint. The inside… is a different story."

"Oh God." I dreaded thinking about how much all the materials were going to set me and Alyssa back.

"Yeah, it needs to be repinned, most of your hardwood floors need to be replaced and then the cracked plaster has to be ripped down and all new sheets put up." My shoulders dropped. I hadn't realized how much work really needed to be done. "Hey don't fret, we're here and in a few weeks it will look like a new dwelling." Garth patted my shoulder before pulling me into his side.

"It's not that, it's the money." They had no idea how much I was struggling. Between paying off the house, the shop rent, and my car, I barely had anything saved for a rainy day and most definitely not for renovations. I had thought about opening the flower stall on Sundays but then I wouldn't have any down time, and recently my friends had been discussing taking another day off! I just couldn't do it. Mondays and Sundays were my weekends because that was all I could afford to take off.

"Hey, it's all good. We'll get this done. I mean, I'll try to help as much as I can, but I gotta find a new apartment to rent and then work."

My head snapped up. "You're looking for a room to rent?"

"Yeah, my landlord is selling, so I have a few wee…"

"Move in here," I cut him off.

He rubbed at his neck, looking a little unsure about the offer "Well…"

"Well what? We get along great and Alyssa is getting married so I have a spare room. You could help me out around here and in return I'll be the greatest roomie ever. It's perfect… right?"

After only a few seconds of contemplation, Garth smiled and stuck his hand out. "Guess I'm moving in, roomie," he winked.

I was so excited as I turned to continue my trek inside that I almost fell right over another tool box. And my new roommate saved the day by catching my arm as I went over. Didn't save me from the bruise my shin was going to sport the next day though.

"Hey, Flynn," I said as I came up beside him and knelt down.

"Hey… what happened to you?" he asked as he reached up and pulled some grass from my hair. "Oh, I had a run in with one of your tool box thingys. So, these are the rotten floor boards hey?"

"Sure are, but nothing that can't be fixed."

He looked so different in dirty work clothes, so casual… I liked it. Actually, I thought work boots and faded jeans suited him more than the dress shoes and button-up collared shirts he usually wore.

"This house has good bones so before long we'll have it looking as good as new," he assured.

I stood up and walked around him towards the kitchen counter and placed Hudson's bouquet of flowers down along with the take-out I had grabbed on the way for them. Just hoped it was still edible since the white boxes were a little crushed from my weight falling on them. "I bought you all Chinese, I hope that's —" Flynn was up immediately and rummaging through the plastic shopping bag before I could finish my sentence. I loved how he felt at home here.

"Guys, dinner!" I called out in the hopes my voice reached the ears of Garth and Hudson. "Oh guess what?" I said to Flynn, as I reached for some bowls from the cupboard.

"What?"

"Garth is moving in here!"

CHAPTER SIX

Hudson

HE'S WHAT! Oh heck no…

"Isn't that great?" she went on smiling at Garth as he entered the kitchen behind me.

Yeah, and there was my best friend looking all proud of himself. "What about Alyssa?" I questioned. No one answered my question. I doubt they even heard it, all hopped up on all the happiness.

"I think it's a great idea," Flynn replied as he dug into the Chinese food containers. "Lyss and I have been talking about moving into one of my rental properties and making it home, so you can move out of the main house and into the bungalow if you want." He pointed his fork my way.

"Gee thanks," I gritted my teeth and glared at him.

"Well, I'm relieved this opportunity dropped into my lap. Means I don't have to keep looking for a new place," Garth added as he shoved food into his mouth and winked towards Savannah.

I walked over to the counter where he was sitting and punched him in the arm. "Yeah, it's a great idea." He looked up at me and caught the look of displeasure I was throwing his way.

"And he can help me get this place into shape and I won't be alone."

"What's going on? What have I missed?" Willow asked as she entered the kitchen.

Thank God she arrived when she did. Maybe she could talk some sense into her friend. It was also a bonus that she couldn't stand Garth on the best of days.

Garth got up from his seat and walked towards her. "Hey, beautiful," he puckered his lips.

She pushed his face away from hers, with a look of disgust. "Keep dreaming, buddy."

He laughed, "Oh I will. Every night, baby."

"Garth is moving in," Savannah informed her as she held a bowl towards her friend.

"Lord help you, girl, you've gone and lost your mind!" she balked as she grabbed the bowl.

"Ouch!" Garth rubbed at his chest as if the statement hurt him. His face told a different story—one of delight.

"Oh stop it. I think it's a perfect plan and I'm going with it," Sav waved off her friend's comment.

"So when do you plan on moving in?" Flynn cut in,

and my brief window of hope that Willow would talk some sense into the situation vanished.

"Well, I gotta be out in a few weeks."

Flynn nodded. "Okay, I'll talk to Alyssa and we can make arrangements to get her stuff moved out in time."

With that, my unspoken disappointment remained unspoken. Didn't mean I wasn't going to rip into my so-called friend once we left the property though.

We packed up and Garth left ahead to wait for me in the truck.

"Thanks so much for working on the house today. I really appreciate it." Savannah leaned against the front door seeing me out as I placed on my boots.

I stood back to full height and looked down at her angelic face. "Of course, I'll be in and out quite a bit. Alyssa gave me the spare key. I hope you don't mind."

She touched my arm. "Of course not. You're welcome here whenever you like, even when you're not working on the house. You know that, right?"

I think I died and went to heaven as she gave me the open invitation to visit anytime.

"Oh, hang on…" She rushed inside and came back holding a bouquet of flowers. "For your grandmother."

I took them from her outstretched hand. "Yeah… about that." *Should I tell her the truth and quite possibly ruin a perfect moment?* "Well, thanks for that." I held them up, then nodded. Garth beeped the horn and I turned to glare at him. "I guess I should be going."

"Yeah, I guess you should be," Sav replied, a small sigh at the end.

Okay, so I didn't want to read too much into that sigh but I did. Was she sighing because I was leaving or because she was going to be in a quiet house alone? Yeah, I wasn't going to get my hopes up.

I said goodbye once more and climbed into the truck. The moment I reversed out the driveway, I reached over and hit Garth in the arm again.

"What the heck? What's gotten into you?"

"You're moving in with her!"

"Well, yeah. What's so wrong with that?" he shrugged, looking at me with that clueless face of his. *Was he serious?*

"Why don't you move into the bungalow and I'll stay in the house. Of all the people you had to go and room with it had to be the woman I'm crushing on!"

"Ah yeah, thanks for the offer of living with you and your old man, but I'm gonna have to say no. I want to live there with Sav, and look at it this way, once the renovations are done you don't need to make excuses to pop around cause your best friend is there," he said and pointed to himself. He had a point no matter how much I hated the thought of them living together. "Plus, you still gotta crawl your ass out of the friend zone man," Garth laughed as he put his foot up on the dashboard, shaking his head with amusement.

Yeah, I did.

CHAPTER SEVEN

S avannah

"Morning, Amy," I waved as I wandered past to go speak to Willow. It was still strange not seeing Alyssa in the candy shop. If I was being honest, I hated it, but I also needed to come to the realization people moved on. They didn't stay in one place; if that happened, then there was no progress, no drive to achieve the next thing. Still… I missed her.

"Will, I need a favor," I leaned against her front counter as she passed a coffee cup to the customer beside me.

"What's that, chick?" she smiled as she too leaned.

"I need you to help me cook something for dinner tonight."

"Ha! What you mean is you need *me* to cook for

you," she waggled her finger in front of my face.

"No… I mean I want to cook something but it has to be easy to follow and minimum ingredients, but still delicious."

"You're really serious?" she eyed me. I could already see that in her mind my attempt would be a disaster. But once I sent her the photos proving I cannot screw up a meal, she would eat her thoughts right back up.

"Yeah, I'm serious."

"Okay, I'll bring a recipe card over to you once the traffic dies a little, then we can quickly go grab ingredients."

"Thank you, I really appreciate it!" I clapped my hands together in elation.

"So, what's the special occasion?"

"Oh nothing, just want to make a nice meal for Garth and Hudson." I swore she leaned even closer as I said that.

"Ah… okay, I get it. Impress the men, or… one man?"

I waved her off. "Stop it."

"So, which one do you like? Please tell me it's not Garth."

I rolled my eyes and giggled. "I do not have a crush on my new roommate."

Yes, Garth had moved in the week before and it turned out that was the best decision I ever made. He was a great roomie, who had me laughing often, cleaned up after himself, and even put the toilet seat down. I could just tell we were going to be fast friends.

Even though we were kind of friends already, we had moved to a whole new level. And boy, did he have it bad for Willow. Poor guy didn't realize the climb he had ahead if he ever wanted Will to take him seriously as a potential boyfriend.

"So it's Hudson. I knew it! And damn, he is one fine specimen."

"It's not Hudson either, I mean I don't look at him that way." *Did I look at him that way?* My thoughts felt complicated when it came to him. I had stopped talking about it to the girls knowing they were sick of it, but there was a huge piece of me that still longed for Chris. Yeah, he had broken my heart more times than I could count, but he had also made me promises—those of a life together—and I had envisioned every moment over the years. And why did he keep returning if he didn't love me? And why did I keep allowing a man I was no longer with to still take up space in my life? Alyssa was moving forward, Willow was moving forward, and I needed to start thinking about doing the same.

As soon as I arrived home I got straight to work by placing all of the ingredients out on the kitchen counter. It was just a simple pasta salad, seeing as Hudson didn't eat meat. The recipe was so easy I could have scoffed at its simplicity! I was even going to attempt dessert, which was just apple slices cooked in cinnamon and sugar with ice cream on top. So what I wanted to know was how in the world I managed to still screw it up and overcook the pasta and burn the apples to the bottom of the saucepan if it was so damn easy!

Still, I dished up the pasta and placed it on the table with a loaf of garlic bread. I heard the truck pull into the driveway and the sound of two doors closing, dreading what they would think about dinner. Hudson picked Garth up most mornings, figuring it was just easier to travel together, and dropped him off every night. The renovations were well under way with just painting left to do. My house's foundation was now level and the walls were crack free.

The front door opened. "Woah, what's on fire?" Garth asked as he walked into the dining room and looked at the table. "Aww, you cooked dinner! You're the best cause I'm starving." He kissed my cheek as he dropped his work cooler on the kitchen counter and headed for the table. Hudson stood near the entryway.

"I… ah, made pasta salad for dinner in case you wanted to maybe stay and eat," I threw the idea out to Hudson feeling quite nervous. I didn't know why I felt that way since he had stayed for dinner half a dozen times already.

He smiled and my legs almost gave way. I didn't like these new feelings that had been stirring more and more of late.

"You cooked vegan for me?"

"Well, sort of, I mean yes, but I did cook meat for Garth, too." I looked over and watched my roommate pick up one of the lamb chops.

"So, I think I've figured out where the burnt smell came from."

He placed the chop back on his plate and I laughed. I couldn't help it. Walking over to the dining table I pointed at him. "I told you I couldn't cook. But no… you said, 'Everyone can cook, Sav, everyone!' Well buddy, enjoy every mouthful of those chops," I smirked in warning. Oh yeah, I was going to watch him choke those down with a grimace on his face.

"Well I'm sure your pasta salad is going to be amazing," Hudson complimented as he reached for the bowl and dished himself a plate.

I unwrapped the garlic bread and place it down front of him. I didn't dare eat until I knew what Hudson thought. He took his first mouthful and smiled as he began to chew. Then his chewing slowed down, and I watched as he tried to keep the smile on his face. He swallowed and I could see it was a hard feat for him to do.

"What's wrong with it?

"Did you put vinegar in it?"

I nodded. "Yeah. The recipe said to add vinegar, oil, parmesan cheese and all that other stuff. So I may not have had oil or parmesan, and I may have overcooked the pasta… a lot, but it still tastes nice with all the nuts, peppers, and legumes, right?" I reached for the pasta and put some on my fork, taking a small mouthful. *Oh God, it was awful.* All I could taste was mush and vinegar! So much vinegar. I spat it out.

"Why did you swallow that?" I pointed at Hudson.

"Because you made it," he said, and I think my heart melted a little.

"Well you're mad! Here, eat the garlic bread. I didn't make it, just baked it." I broke some off for him and handed it to him. "Just kind of chew around the bottom, that part is a little burnt."

Garth pushed his plate forward. "So… what's for dessert?" I sighed. Standing up, I walked over to the cook top and held up the scorched saucepan. "I feel like I just competed in an episode of *Nailed It*," I laughed. "What I envisioned somehow didn't exactly turn out the same way."

Hudson got up from the table and walked towards me. He took the saucepan from my hands and placed it back on the stove. His body was so close as he ran his hands along my arms. "Have you still got apples?" he asked looking down at me. I nodded my mouth dry. "Okay, well let's try it again, only an easier way and do it together." I nodded again. Seems that was the only thing I was capable of in that moment.

"Well, while you two do that, I'll go get pizza. Be back soon." Garth took off out the door.

We got to work and Hudson showed me how easy it was to cook apples with cinnamon using the microwave and then add the ice cream on top.

Garth finally returned with edible food, and thankfully dinner was saved.

"Well I'm off to bed, got a big day tomorrow. Night guys," Garth said after a time, as he got up from the sofa. And then… it was just Hudson and me.

CHAPTER EIGHT

*H*udson

"Well I should be going, too." I stood up from the sofa I had been sitting on next to Sav. She reached out, as if trying to catch me and then pulled her arm back like she couldn't quite believe she had done that.

"Oh, you don't have to leave. I mean, I'm not tired or anything."

I raised my brows a little in shock at the situation I found myself in with no effort on my part. "So, are you saying you want me to stay or are you just being nice?" *Please say you want me to stay.*

She shyly smiled up at me. "No, I want you to stay." And that was all it took for me to slowly seat myself down once again.

She turned her body and tucked her legs into the sofa cushion. "So, tell me about you, Hudson."

"What do you want to know, Savannah?" I turned also and rested my elbow on top of the sofa.

She shrugged. "Anything, everything. But make it interesting," she smiled over at me.

I nodded as I thought about where to start. "I love snow globes."

Her mouth dropped into an open grin. "Ah, what?"

"Well, you know I'm a man who still lives at home, by choice I might add, and I'm not ashamed of that. You know my family, my job, and you've started meeting my friends. But the one thing you didn't know was that I like to collect snow globes."

"Wow, well there you go, I was not expecting that. So… is it like when people go away they bring you one back or is it snow globes in general?"

"In general," I laughed as my eyes remained fixated on hers. "My mother used to buy them for me when I was little. There was no occasion. So when she went shopping and found one she thought I would like, she would bring it home and leave it on my desk. I guess, it's just something I continue because it reminds me of her, a connection of some sort."

"Do you miss her? I mean, of course you miss her that was a stupid question to ask. Just ignore me," she blushed and broke our eye contact.

All I wanted her to do was turn her head and look at me once more so I continued to talk. "She's been gone for a few years now. I still think of her, but I also feel relieved because I know she's not in pain from the cancer anymore. And I always have my snow globes," I wiggled my brows, and she covered her mouth trying to cut off the giggle that wanted to break loose.

"What about you? What don't I know about you?" I threw the questions her way. And God, did I want to know every tiny thing about that woman and what made her tick.

She tapped at her chin as she thought about where to start. "Well, I don't really have any family. I mean, I have my mom, but she lives in Boston and the moment I was 16 she kicked me out."

"I'm sorry," I immediately replied and reached out to take her hand in mine. I waited for her to pull it back, so you can imagine my surprise when she just squeezed it tighter and kept hold.

"Oh don't be. We were never close. She loved to party, and well I was the parent. Anyway, I got on a bus with my suitcase and didn't know where I was going to get off, but then I walked into a diner here in Seattle and Alyssa served me. From that day forward, she got me a job there and we moved in together."

"That's how you two met?" I asked.

She nodded, and the sweetest reminiscing smile adorned her face. "Yeah, that's when I met my best friend, and we loved working in the diner, but I knew I wanted to be a florist, so one day I saw an ad in the paper for an apprenticeship at Daisies and got the job. Anyway, as time went on, Alyssa bought Just as Sweet, and a few months after she took over she heard the shop next to her was going up for lease. She managed to wrangle it for me and I started my own flower business. And… that's my story."

I could tell there was more to her story but I figured if she ever wanted me to know she would tell me. "So, speaking of your flower shop, I have a confession."

She let go of my hand, and instantly I missed her warmth. She sat back as if she was preparing herself for bad news, like I was going to hurt her in some way. For a moment I questioned whether I should own up at all. But I knew I had to if I wanted to have anything with Sav. I needed to be honest.

"I don't really buy flowers every week for my grandmother because, well, she died a really long time ago." I watched as her mouth flopped open and thoughts swam in her eyes, but after a short time I watched as her head tilted and one side of her mouth lifted in my direction.

"Did you buy flowers just so you could see me?"

Reaching a hand up I scratched at my beard nervously. "Ah yeah, I did. And in case you haven't figured it out yet, I like you a lot, Savannah."

Her eyes widened, yet still she never moved them away from mine. I thought I had blown it. I stood up to leave when she didn't say anything for a good while. "So, I'm going to leave you with that admission, and hopefully we can talk about it another day."

I opened the front door but then heard her call back to me.

"Wait, Hudson. " I turned, and there she was,

walking down the hallway towards me . "I don't know what I feel. I mean, it's complicated. But I do… feel things… for you. I just—"

That was all I needed to hear in that moment. Leaning down, I placed my lips on hers and cut off her rambling. And oh boy it worked. As our lips melded and her warm sweet taste entered my mouth, I truly thought I had died and gone to heaven. She lifted her arms up to wrap them around my shoulders and I caught them and broke the kiss. I could have stayed there making out all night, but something told me not to rush whatever was between us. So, reluctantly, I stepped back.

"We'll talk about whatever is happening between us later. Night, beautiful," I finished and leaned down to kiss the tip of her nose.

"Ah yeah… things… talk." She mumbled as she raised a hand to her lips.

God, she was adorable.

CHAPTER NINE

Savannah

"WHAT! HE KISSED YOU!" Alyssa squealed with delight at a deafening level.

"Shh! You don't have to let the entire restaurant know I just had the best damn kiss of my life," I growled and yet whispered at the same time, giving her all sorts of looks.

"Well, I think it's about time, and I also think it is a great idea for us to do lunch more often," Willow added as she took a sip of her white wine.

I agreed by nodding, but inside I was panicking. I was struggling a little to stay ahead of the bills, seeing as the shop rent had been raised again. But I had finally done what Alyssa had suggested and began to sell my jewelry in the store. It had been going well and had given me another idea… Etsy! Yeah, I was in the middle of setting up my very own online shop and I hoped it was going to be a hit. I wasn't ready to tell anyone about it just yet in case it was a total bust.

"Okay, so I know I said I wasn't going to talk wedding stuff today, but I was really hoping we could sneak in a dress shop visit for your bridesmaid dresses… please," Alyssa brought her hands up in front of her as if praying.

"Gah," Willow pretended to barf before adding. "You better not put us in ruffles."

Alyssa dropped her hands to the table. "If you keep rolling your eyes at me, I may do just that," she warned our friend.

"Well, I love the whole wedding thing, and if dress shopping makes you happy, then dress shopping we shall do," I smiled over at Alyssa. I knew how stressed she had become of late, with trying to run her businesses, spend time with us and Flynn, and planning an entire wedding—it was wearing on her. But she was amazing and unless you knew her well, you wouldn't have thought she was close to her breaking point.

"Thank you, Sav, and seeing as you are so willing to accommodate me, would you mind helping Willow organize the bachelorette party because I don't trust her and I explicitly said no strippers." She turned to glare at our friend again.

"And I said I won't hire any strippers," she glared right back. The moment Alyssa broke eye contact with her, she turned her head and winked at me.

Oh Lord…

FINISHING OUR LUNCH, we left the restaurant and headed straight to the bridal store. After some major no-no moments, I eventually tried on a pale green knee-length dress with a beautiful cream satin ribbon around the waist and a strapless bodice, paired with diamante heels.

"Oh, it's beautiful," I said as I stepped out of the changing room and spun in front of the shop mirror.

Willow walked out from her changing room barefoot and half zipped up. "I look too… girly."

Alyssa got up from her chair and walked over to her. "No, you look adorable and sweet and…"

"Yeah, it's not me," Will shook her head.

"Yes, it is and you are going to love it because I think these are the dresses ladies," Alyssa clapped in excitement.

I clapped along, joining in the moment, and walked over to grab a glass of champagne from the small table by the shop window. I shouldn't have glanced up from the table and out the shop window while taking a sip from the flute because the moment I did my eyes landed on the one person they should have never looked at again—Chris. He stopped in shock at also seeing me. I spat the entire contents all over the glass and somehow inhaled at the same time bringing on a spat of choking for air. Clutching at my chest while coughing, I turned and walked back to the changing room. When I heard the bell above the front door, I froze.

"Sav?"

Damn it! My nerves were shot, my heart beating a million miles a minute.

"Buzz off, Chris," Willow barked as she popped her head out from behind the curtain.

"I, ah…" he looked from me to her.

I swiveled around to face him. "Hey there," I gave a small wave.

"Wow, um… it's great to see you," he said.

"Ha!" I heard Willow scoff in the dressing room next to me.

"So I'm just going to go… help Willow get out of her dress," Alyssa made the excuse and quickly disappeared behind the curtain and out of sight.

"Don't you dare leave that jerk alone with Sav. You know the games he plays," Willow growled and I looked over to see the curtain moving as if someone was trying to get out. Then the sounds of a large thud reverberated from the room as legs popped out from the bottom. Obviously, Alyssa had won the tackle and I rolled my eyes.

"Enough, Will. I'm a big girl," I stated, right before I walked over to stand in front of Chris.

"So, what are you doing here?" he asked.

"Oh, Alyssa is getting married in a couple of months," I pointed back at the curtain.

"Wow, well congrats, Lyss."

"Thanks!" she called out.

As a moment of silence fell between us, I struggled to come up with anything to say. Chris was still just as handsome as ever, and somehow even in old age I thought he would still look mighty fine. Made me wish he had an ugly personality, but that wasn't the case. He had never been mean to me—with his words. It was his action of always leaving me when he felt he needed more that was cruel.

"How's business?" he managed to pull me from my thoughts.

"It's going really well. Actually, life is going really well. All in all, I'm..."

"Well," he spoke for me and I blushed with embarrassment. "Ah, you look great by the way. I forgot just how beautiful you are." *Oh Lord, his words always got me.* "So, we should catch up. I mean if you want to. I would really love that," he put out there.

For the briefest of moments I contemplated saying yes. I mean, this was the moment I had been longing for, right? Then the face of a man who had been starring in my nightly dreams appeared in my mind. *Hudson.*

I shook my head. "Yeah, no. I don't think that's a good idea, Chris."

"Damn straight!" I heard Willow agree.

"Will would you shut it!" I snapped.

For a moment Chris seemed almost shocked that I had turned him down. Guess it would have been a shock, seeing as every other time he came crawling back, there I was with forgiveness and open arms. *God, I was pathetic.*

But then he nodded. "Well, it was really great seeing you," he said and gave me that smile that always did terrible things to my insides.

I held it together long enough to watch him walk away and leave the store. The moment he was out of eye sight, I lost it. "Oh God, where's my purse?" I went looking for it.

"Why what's wrong?" Alyssa asked worriedly as she burst out from behind the room's curtain.

"I need my bag." The moment I saw it sitting next to the chair Alyssa had been sitting on earlier, I sat down and pulled it onto my lap and began rummaging through it. I pulled out my little baggie of supplies with a sigh of relief.

"You're going to start making bracelets in the middle of the bridal store?" Willow balked.

"No, I'm going to make a necklace." My hands were shaky as I began pulling beads out as I tried to get them onto the chain.

"See and this is why you can never catch up with him. Look at what it does to you," Willow growled.

"Oh God, he really does cause me a world of anxiety," I admitted.

"Talk to me," Alyssa crouched down and placed her hands on mine, stilling them.

"He's the first man I ever loved. I... it hurts to see someone you had your life planned out with just walking through the world as if nothing happened. As if no one was broken by his choices."

"He's a jerk!"

"Will…" Alyssa warned.

"No, she needs to hear this. How many times has he broken your heart? How many times has he walked away and then come crawling back?"

"But he wasn't ever mean. He just…" I tried to defend him, but I had no case.

"I agree with Willow. I'm sorry, sweetheart, but he was selfish. Only thinking about what he wanted, never what you wanted."

"I know you're both right. I just don't know how to move on. I mean no, that's not true. I do know how to move on, I'm just afraid."

Willow grabbed the beads from my hands along with my handbag and threw them back in. "Woman, get out there and damn well kiss that Hudson again. Go on some dates, then you'll realize there are men out there that will adore and love you and appreciate those God given curve of yours."

I didn't want to admit it, but that was one heck of a pep talk. It was so damn good it had me rising from my seat with fire in my belly.

"Yeah, you're right. I need to move on for good and be appreciated!" I agreed with her. That didn't mean it was going to be easy to do.

CHAPTER TEN

*H*udson

As I was sitting out on the back deck enjoying my breakfast while wondering whether I should call Savannah to see if she had plans for this Sunday morning, I heard my phone buzzing. Looking down at the illuminated screen, Garth's name stared back at me. Before hello even left my mouth he was talking.

"Dude, something is up with Savannah." I rose from my seat at the panic in his voice.

"What is it? Is she okay?" As I asked I was already in mission mode and heading inside the house to grab my keys.

"Well, yeah I guess, but she's singing songs and cleaning my room. Oh, and did I mention she's tone deaf and that she's cleaning my room!"

I stopped at the kitchen counter my hand on my keys. "Why is she cleaning your room?"

"I don't know, I think she's been up since the crack of dawn and done the entire house twice over and she says once she's finished, we're going to the nursery for plant shopping."

"Yeah… you've lost me," I shook my head confused by the call.

"Okay, so since I moved in, Savannah does not clean. I mean she does, but not like this. *This* is scary!"

Smiling to myself, I was thinking my boy was exaggerating her actions.

"I know you think I'm acting stupid about this, Hudson, but I'm not! Come over and see for yourself!" he yelled before hanging up on me.

I got in my truck and called Alyssa, placing my phone onto Bluetooth. If anyone knew Savannah's behavior it would be my future sister-in-law. The moment she answered I asked her straight. "Why is Savannah cleaning and singing?"

"Oh God," she sighed into the phone. "She's self-empowering."

"What?" I asked confused about the sentence.

"Okay, so my mother, as you know, is a self-love guru or whatever. Anyway, she gave Savannah these coping techniques. One is to make something to distract and calm your energy, which is why she makes bracelets. The other is to tackle the things that hold you back from moving on, clean out your spaces and declutter. So… she's essentially organizing and decluttering her life."

"Okay, so I hear what you're saying, sort of. So what does this mean? Is it something we should worry about or do we just let her go on with the whole decluttering thing she's doing?"

"It means she's struggling big time."

"Well, I'm on my way over there."

"Want me to meet you?" she offered.

"Do I need to have you there?" I was seriously concerned with what I was about to walk into.

Alyssa laughed. "You know what? If you really want to be there for her, then I am handing you the reins. Take her out, distract her… work your magic and make her feel good about herself."

"Okay, done. Wish me luck," I replied a little uncertain as to whether I could pull it off. *Be the man she needed, the friend if that was what was called for.*

"You won't need it Hudson. You're a great guy and Savannah is one-of-a-kind, she's just a little broken but nothing that can't be fixed with a little glue."

I hung up with Alyssa and prepared for whatever situation I was heading into.

"LOOK—CRAZY!" he pointed into his bedroom where Alyssa sat on the floor at the foot of his bed, folding his underwear into the bottom drawer of his tall dresser. "She's folding my *briefs,* man. And if I have to hear her sing Rhianna's song 'Umbrella' one more time I'm going to put a whole in her freshly-painted hallway wall," he groaned in frustration.

She was a beauty, but I had to admit her singing voice wasn't her best quality. It was downright awful, as much as I hated to admit it.

"Hey, beautiful, how you feeling today?" I asked as I approached her, and crouched down beside her.

She looked over at me and immediately stopped singing. I wished I could say she let go of my friend's underwear, but hey, progress was a process.

"Hi, Huddy. That's my new nickname for you. Do you like it?"

No, I didn't but I wasn't about to wipe that smile off her face. "I'm sure it will grow on me."

"Well, what about Hud? Or son? Or… handsome, but then that's kind of longer than your name really is…"

"How about you drop Garth's briefs and we can go somewhere to discuss my new nickname."

She raised an eyebrow and bit at her lip. "What are you offering? I'm intrigued at your proposal."

Kill. Me. Now. If she bit her lip a moment longer, I was unsure if I could hold myself back from pushing her to the floor and finishing what we started last week. I cleared my throat, "How about ice cream?" And just like that the underwear was thrown and Sav was on her feet.

"Let me just grab my sunglasses and I'll be ready to

go." She stopped in front of Garth and tapped his nose. "You are welcome."

"For what?" he looked down at her confused.

"For me literally cleaning your entire room, except the final drawer."

He laughed, "Yeah well, next time, do you mind going one step further and ironing my underwear just how I like it?" I hit him up the side of the head as I followed Sav out, shooting daggers his way and a silent *careful buddy!*

Another fun fact I only found out was, apparently, Savannah loved ice cream and she wasn't afraid to drag me back into the store and order a second cone with two scoops of coconut and boysenberry. And I think I fell a little more for her, as I leaned forward and kissed the little bit of left over ice cream from the side of her top lip. It was short and sweet, but when I pulled back and waited for her eyes to open, my heart burst from the mere fact I wasn't the only one affected by the feelings that were growing between us.

"Ready for our next adventure?" I asked and her eyes popped open.

"What does our next adventure hold?"

Reaching down I placed my hand in hers and pulled her towards the dock. "I thought we could take a ferry ride around Seattle. I mean, if that's something you would like."

She squeezed my hand and moved in closer to my side. "I think that sounds perfect."

Savannah closed her eyes as the sea air streamed past her face.

"So what's going on, Sav? You seemed pretty determined to clean the house from top to bottom today, kind of scared Garth there for a moment." I faced her as I leaned against the boat's railing. She opened her eyes and looked at me confused. "Is it about the other day, me kissing you?"

"Oh no, I… liked that a lot," she assured me and I took a much needed breath. "It's complicated," she sighed as she mimicked my stance and leaned against the railing also.

"I'm all ears."

"I don't think you want to hear all of my woes, Hudson."

I shrugged, "Try me."

"Okay, but don't say I didn't warn you. I had a boyfriend, Chris Carlton. He… kind of has this habit of breaking my heart. You see, we've been on and off seven times the past six years. Well, I should say he left me and broke my heart coming up on almost a year and a half ago now. I may have had a hard time dealing with that."

She was right, I didn't know if I wanted to hear about her ex, but she had warned me and I still stupidly jumped in. "Do you still love him?"

She shook her head. "No, I… like I said, it's complicated. You see, before I met you there was always this sliver of hope that he would come back. That I would finally be good enough for him. I tried to lose weight for a while thinking that he might have wanted someone beautiful on his arm, and then he would love me. I know it all sounds crazy. But sometimes, I wonder if I loved him or was in love with the idea of being in love."

I knew the guy she was talking about. Well, not knew him personally, but had seen him on those cheesy car ads for his business, and I hated to admit it but I could see the attraction. I myself almost bought a truck simply because he said you can't buy from just anyone, you need to buy from the best!

"I can't tell you what to do or how to move on, Sav. You know how I feel about you, but if you just need a friend right now, then I'll be that, too."

It would kill me to have to go back into the friend zone, but if that's what she needed then I would do that because I would do anything to make her happy.

She leaned in and wrapped her arms about my waist. "I like you too, and… I don't want to be stuck there, in the past, waiting for the wrong thing. I want to be happy, you know?"

Placing my thumb on her chin, I tilted her face up to see me say the next words. "You make me happy, beautiful, and I hope I get to do the same for you."

Reaching up on her tiptoes, she placed her lips against mine, and I closed my eyes, wanting to feel every moment of the sweet gesture she was offering me. No pressure, just her initiating and wanting me as much as I wanted her. She had become my new home.

CHAPTER ELEVEN

$\mathcal{S}$avannah

"OH MY, why am I so nervous?" I looked down at my pink polka dot dress again and wiped at the creases that weren't really there. "I mean, this I weird, right? I know you're dad and I'm pretty sure he loves me and I've been here many times before!"

"Shh," Hudson chuckled as he leaned down to kiss me.

More like shut me up but whatever the reason it worked. Oh boy, did it work. His lips did crazy things to me, rendering me speechless at the best of times. And don't even get me started on how relaxing it was to play with his beard. It was my new obsession for sure.

"Relax, beautiful, it's just dinner." He entwined our fingers, as he opened up the front door and led me in.

"Yeah but it's like, official, meet the folks kind of heavy crazy stuff! There's a lot of pressure here."

He burst into laughter as he pulled me through the house. "Dad, we're here," he called out, still trying to calm the giggles he had going. I didn't think meeting his father as his girlfriend was all that funny. I felt extreme pressure, even if I did know the man.

"You're here. Welcome, Savannah," Andy greeted me as Hudson pulled me into the kitchen.

"Hey, Mr. Colson, thanks for having me tonight," I replied as he walked over and kissed my cheek.

"Always Andy, and always welcome, my dear. Now, can you two help me take these dishes to the dining table?" he asked as he reached for the salad bowl.

"Of course," I replied, letting go of Hudson's hand and grabbing the creamy potato bake.

Dinner was delicious. At first, I wondered as I was dishing up my plate whether I would even be able to stomach anything, being as nervous as I was. But a few minutes into eating, I relaxed. It was as comfortable as every other time I had been there; I just once again overreacted about things. As the talk turned to work and business between father and son, I zoned out as I thought about the past few weeks. It had been a dream come true, and yeah, I had fallen for Hudson Colson in a big way. Often, I would find myself just staring at him and shaking my head and thinking, *How did I not notice him sooner?* Sure, I noticed him, but I never thought I would be head over heels. He took me out all the time, and other times he just came over to hang out or watch a movie. We never really got to the movie part as other things kept us happily distracted. I wanted to spend every waking and sleeping moment with him. I also hadn't made a single piece of jewelry in weeks! Still, there was a secret I was keeping, and I didn't know whether to tell him or not. Not at dinner of course, but… well, I would think about it later.

My phone went off and pulled me out of my thoughts. Pulling it from my dress pocket, I looked at the caller ID under the table. *Damn it!* "Can you just excuse me for a second?" I asked holding up a finger as I stood from my chair.

Hudson nodded, a look on his face that was asking. *All ok?* I smiled reassuringly and walked out into the hallway. The phone began to ring again and I answered it, a bite in my tone. "I told you stop calling. Lose my number."

"We have to talk Sav. Please?" Chris pleaded.

"I'm at my boyfriend's house," I growled and hung up, hoping the word "boyfriend" would shut these phone calls down for good.

"Everything all right?" Hudson rounded the corner and startled me.

I swung around to face him and held the phone behind my back blindly pressing the off button to turn the stupid thing off. "Yeah, just Willow," I lied to him right before placing my hand in his and leading him back to the dining table to finish dinner.

"So have you been over to Flynn and Alyssa's new place yet?" Andy asked me as I took my seat.

"Have I ever! First, they're only like 5 minutes away from me and two, they have a pool."

"We have a pool here you know," Hudson reminded me.

"Yeah but I mean… I don't think your dad…" I pointed.

He lifted his hands. "No, by all means, my home is your home and I would love nothing more than to have you here. I'm an old man now, but I love family, and you, my dear, are family."

I clutched at my chest, the sentiment squeezing at my heart. I didn't have family of my own, except Alyssa and Willow. The statement meant more to me than Mr. Colson knew.

"Why are you so sweet?" I asked. "Must be where Hudson gets it from."

He laughed. "No, darling, I've just mellowed out in my old age, and I love having family around. So please, come and go as you choose."

After staying and talking until almost midnight, I said my goodbyes and Hudson drove me home. "You know I could have driven myself, right? That way you didn't have to leave the house."

"Are you kidding? I love picking up my girl."

Oh God, that statement did something to me and had me squirming in my seat as my entire body lit up. *His girl!* My phone rang again, and I just knew I never should have switched it back on before leaving Mr. Colson's.

"You going to answer it?" Hudson glanced over at me.

"No, it's just Willow annoying me again." I was such a liar! But I wasn't ready to tell him, if I was ever going to tell him at all. Why worry him when Chris calling meant nothing. No, I was going to handle this myself.

"Want me to walk you in?" he offered as he pulled the truck into my driveway.

I leaned over and kissed him on those delectable lips of his, letting our mouths linger on one another's a few seconds. Reluctantly, I pulled away and opened my eyes. "No, but… maybe tomorrow?" I raised a brow.

"I'll be here."

I climbed out of the truck before I changed my mind and wound up crawling over the handbrake for a make-out session. "Great, I'll order takeout."

He smiled, "I can cook you know."

"Okay then you can cook for us. Yes, Garth included." I rolled my eyes, knowing Hudson had something to say about it.

"Of course," he grumbled.

"Night," I blew him one last kiss before running to the front door.

Dropping my bag on the hallway table, Garth called out from the living room, "Have a good night?"

I walked in to see him sitting on the sofa. "I had a great night. Andy is like the sweetest gentleman ever!" I told him as I plopped down on the sofa beside him and placed my feet across his lap. "I need you to rub them, I wore heels and I don't know why I tortured my feet like that."

He began kneading them. "Yeah, why did you? Not like you haven't met Andy before."

"Yeah I know, I just wanted to make… I don't know. I just wanted to look nice."

"Well, you always look nice, and Hudson is smitten."

I couldn't help the grin that erupted on my face. "Yeah I know, I feel the same." Garth removed a hand from my legs and pulled out his phone.

"What did you take a snap of my legs for?"

"To piss Hudson off. He's gonna be so jealous he isn't the one rubbing your legs," Garth chuckled.

Oh, he was such a stirrer. "You send that and I'm not the one that's gonna be in trouble."

"Too late." It wasn't even ten seconds later, his phone rang. "What's up! Dude, I can't help if your woman can't resist my hands." I reached up and grabbed the phone from him. "Hey."

"What the heck, Sav?"

"Relax, I'm just getting him to rub my legs I shouldn't have worn the heels. Besides, it's Garth."

"Ouch! Those kinds of statements hurt a man," he tried to look emotionally wounded, but couldn't quite seem to drop the smile.

"Yeah, you're right. Okay, have a good night, love you," he hung up and I dropped the phone to my chest.

"What's wrong?" Garth asked as I lay there with my mouth open.

"Um…Hudson just said he loved me."

"Duh! We all kind of know that."

I pulled my legs from him and sat up. "Yeah, but he said he loved me. Maybe he just said it out of habit like, okay bye love you. Or do you think he meant I love you Savannah because you're my world."

The thought was almost too much for me to comprehend. This was huge, and I had no idea what to do with it.

I heard my phone going off again. *Not now!*

CHAPTER TWELVE

*H*udson

I HAD to admit as I sat by the fire at Flynn's new place that I couldn't help feeling disappointed this was the bachelor night he wanted. Could I just say boring! Don't get me wrong, it was a beautiful two-story town-house, complete with pool, games room, and all the trimmings to start a family. Still, we could sit around a fire on the back deck any night of the week. Be that as it may, I kept my mouth shut, seeing as that was what Flynn wanted—a low-key get together with some of our friends chugging some beer with music playing through the portable speaker. Still… boring!

"So, did you end up getting the river ranch for your wedding?" I asked my big bro.

The grin that lit up his face said it all. "Got it all

right! And we're all booked. Oh, and I hope you don't mind we put you, Willow, Sav, and Garth in one five-bedroom cabin, okay?" he eyed me.

"Of course! Can't believe it's only two weeks away though. Time flew by."

"I know, it's crazy. But honestly, it can't come quick enough. I've been wanting to officially make that woman mine since the first moment I saw her." I knew the feeling my brother was talking about. I'd marry Savannah right now, if I knew it wouldn't scare her away. "So how's it all going with Sav?" he asked me as he leaned over his chair and pulled out two more beers, handing me one.

"Yeah, it was going well. I mean, until I told her I loved her on the phone last week. And... well, she's been a little distant since. We went from seeing each other every day to the past few days she's had a 'headache'. Do you think I jumped the gun?"

Flynn shook his head as he downed his beer. "No, I don't. I was full on with Alyssa. You've taken it nice and steady with your girl."

"Dude, what's with this boring ass guys' night? Where are the strippers?" Garth came storming over, looking about as unimpressed as I was feeling. I just loved how he had the balls to say it out loud what I'm sure everyone else was thinking.

"I promised Alyssa none of that."

"Dude, that's crap. Then why do the girls get them?" he demanded to know.

"Ah, they don't. Alyssa was pretty adamant about it being a clean get together."

He pulled his phone out of his back pocket and a few seconds later, Garth turned it around and held it out so we could see the screen. "See. This is Willow's instagram page. And here's the proof that the girls are off their heads, having fun with male dancers, while we sit around a damn fire with our coworkers."

I laughed with amusement. "Well they look like they're having fun."

"Over my dead body," Flynn got up from his seat lightning quick.

"Where you off to? You've been drinking!" I called out as he rushed towards the house. He paused and turned to point at Garth. "Call me a cab. And find out where they're at."

"Now we're talking. Let's go boys. Time to crash the girls' party!" Garth ran after Flynn who had disappeared into the house.

I sat back in my chair. I figured let 'em just have their fun, rite of passage and all. Flynn wasn't as open-minded. Twenty minutes later I found my butt being hauled into a cab and before I knew it, we were walking into the club. Didn't take me long to spot our girls, as tall as I was. Also helped to look for the party of women where one was sporting a pink veil, letting everyone else there know she was a bride-to-be. By the way she was dancing around and knocking into her friends, I could tell Alyssa was long past sober. Willow was next to her dancing with one of the topless waiters. All together there were at least twenty girls there in the bachelorette party. I didn't know any of them except…

"Hudson!" I could just hear my name being called above the music that was blaring through the club. Savannah came running for me, pushing her way through the crowd. When she got close, she jumped and looped her arms around my shoulders, kissing me with fire and catching me off guard. But I caught up pretty damn quick. It sucked she was drunk though.

I broke the kiss, and placed her gently down on her feet. She wasn't letting go though. "You love me! Me," she pointed to herself.

"I do. Maybe not how I was planning to say it, being on the phone and all, but it's true."

She grabbed my cheek and squeezed. "Aww, you're so sweet!"

I looked above Sav's head to see that Garth was trying to pull Willow away from the waiter. She fought him every step of the way, but in the end, Garth won. He threw her over his shoulder and marched towards where Flynn and I were standing. I had no issue with Sav, but Flynn on the other hand was trying to get Alyssa before she climbed on the bar.

"Guys, get your women we're out!" he called above the music.

"I'm telling you. You're messing up my game!" Willow screeched right into Garth's ear.

He flinched before whacking her on the butt. "Sweetheart, there was no game. Trust me, that waiter was relieved to not be woman-handled by you a moment longer!" Willow obviously wasn't happy with that statement as she began to pound into Garth's back. She was a feisty little thing, that was for sure.

Flynn finally had Alyssa around the waist and she was all over him, trying to kiss him while moving her hips in what seemed to be dance moves. I couldn't help but laugh at my sister-in-law. Why the guys were being such alpha males was beyond me. The ladies were just having a good time.

We piled into a minivan taxi, all the while Willow was screaming like a drunken little pixie. "Where to?" I asked everyone, so I could give the driver directions.

"Oh, back to Alyssa and Flynn's so we can go swimming!" Sav clapped. Damn it, even drunk she was adorable. And I hadn't seen her so care-free before.

"No swimming for you, sweetheart," I kissed the tip of her nose, and she sighed as she grabbed my face and began stroking my beard.

"Hey! She can do what she wants, buddy!" Willow leaned forward in her seat, pointing her finger at me. She must have sat too far forward as she fell off it and onto the floor. We waited for her to get up, but a moment later all we heard was her God-awful deep snoring.

"Great! She is literally drooling at my feet," Garth groaned right before pulling out his phone and snapping a picture. "I can't wait to show her these in the morning," he grinned.

"So maybe… just home to my house?" Sav yawned as she slurred her words.

"Yeah, home," I agreed.

"Will you stay with me?" she asked as she nestled her head into my shoulder, still stroking my beard.

I kissed the top of her head. "Sure."

Garth carefully picked Willow up off the cab floor and cradled her to his chest. I could see the way he felt about her, and felt sorry for the guy. As of yet, I had no vibe coming from Willow as to whether she reciprocated his feelings.

The four of us exited, and I turned to look back at Flynn and Lyss. "What are you guys up to? Coming in?"

"Oh, we're going home to have our own… show," Alyssa giggled as she bit at my brother's ear. Yep, too much information for me and not a sight I was going to hang around for.

"Later!" I slid the cab door closed. I walked Savannah inside, her arms tight around my waist. We hadn't even had the chance to close the front door before Garth was standing in front of us in the hallway, his hands on hips.

"We'll, I've tucked Willow in, so I'm gonna take the sofa. And if you hear the sounds of a grizzly through the night, it's just Sleeping Beauty in there!" I laughed, because I could hear her from where I was standing and it was horrid.

"Night, Garthy boy, I'll see you in the mornin'," Savannah said, before grabbing my hand and leading me into her bedroom. Once inside, she let go of my hand and fell face down onto her bed.

"Ah, you okay there?" I asked as I closed the door behind me out of habit. She didn't even answer, the only sound coming from her was the softest of snores. My girl was out cold.

Moving her around on the bed so I could slip in next to her turned out to be a chore. She was not bending at all. I managed to lift her a little to slide on in and placed her head on my chest. I wasn't going to mention in the morning the drool puddle she was creating. Drool or not, she was still perfect to me.

CHAPTER THIRTEEN

Savannah

I HATED HANGOVERS. Like really hated them, and chastised myself for drinking way more than I should have. I knew the limit of what my curvy body could handle, yet I was having so much fun I just kept swallowing the drinks down.

Alyssa had specifically said no strippers, and of course I was at fault for not coming through and working on keeping Willow in check. I promised my best friend I'd help out, but well, Hudson got my attention instead. Overall, the night was a success and once we were there, well that's when things really heated up. Before long, we were pulled up on stage and made a part of the routine, touching places that made us squeal!

I loved every minute of it! But not the hangover, definitely not that.

I could hear Hudson and Garth arguing in the kitchen, as I pulled my body upright from the bed. Reaching into my bedside drawer, I pulled out a hair tie and placed my bed hair up into a messy bun. I didn't even want to look at my reflection and what disaster awaited me in the reflection, so I chose to walk right by my mirror and forced myself to rush out the door before I regretted looking. As I entered the kitchen, it became apparent they weren't yelling at all, just talking really loudly. Or maybe I was just sensitive because I had one heck of a headache.

Sitting down on one of the counter seats, I rested my head against the cool marble surface. "Morning beautiful, how you feeling?"

"Blech," I managed to get out.

"Want some breakfast? I'm cooking pancakes." That made my morning, and I wanted to look up and smile at him, but instead I just raised my thumb. Hudson placed my phone down beside me.

"Oh, Chris called you like ten times. You better call him back," he informed me.

That got my head rising as I reached for the phone and pressed the button. Yep, ten times exactly. I glanced over at Hudson standing in front of the stove. He didn't look upset as he stood there flipping the pancakes, and I wondered why the heck not!

"Yeah, I will. Must be about something important." I

turned the phone to silent. I would deal with Chris later.

Hudson slid a plate piled high with pancakes, and even bacon towards me and my mouth salivated. "You're amazing, you know that?" I said as I leaned over the counter and kissed his lips.

And he really was, I had fallen hard. Like slap me silly this man is to die for hard. For the first time in a really long time, I felt nothing for my ex. The realization dawned on me as I watched Hudson finish up breakfast and begin to wash the skillet. I had moved on and stepped into a place where I was happy. Oh God, I was so happy it hurt. But I needed to confront my past, to end it once and for all with Chris.

"Hey, I helped," Garth added. "I squeezed the oranges." He slid a glass towards me of fresh juice. Damn, I was so preoccupied with my hangover and the handsome boyfriend of mine, I forgot poor Garth was even in the room.

"Well, thank you," I reached up and squeezed Garth's cheek. "You sure did help and I appreciate it," I complimented. He looked like a boy who had been verbally rewarded for doing his chores or something. I actually understood him. He had essentially grown up like me, without much, if any, family at all. He just wanted to be seen and loved. And I had begun to love him dearly.

"Gah! Enough with all the ruckus! I want to die..." Willow whined as she walked into the kitchen with last night's black dress on and her hair stuck to the side of her face. She sat down beside me and grabbed a piece of bacon off my plate.

"You need to stop drinking so much," I laughed, understanding her hangover all too well.

"Well it's fun while I'm buzzed, but you're right, I think my days of partying may be coming to an end," she admitted as she shoved the entire piece of bacon into her mouth. Hudson slid a plate in front of her, and she look up at him in thanks. "I love you," she whispered at him, right before she reached for the maple syrup.

"Does that mean you're ready to settle down?" Garth inquired.

"Stop! I don't feel like dealing with you today," she held up a hand, not looking at him.

"Jeez, a man gives up his bed and this is the thanks he gets." Garth threw his hands up.

"No, you're right. I'll lay off you a bit… this morning at least."

"Really?" he leaned against the counter.

"I said this morning, not tomorrow, and thank you for… looking after me."

Willow glanced his way. "You're welcome." And with that, once again Garth looked like a kid in a candy store as he stared admirably at Willow scoffing down her breakfast. He was so sweet, and smitten over my friend. She, on the other hand, really wasn't giving him an inch. I was surprised because Garth was good-looking and manly, and Willow loved her men. Yet with him, she didn't blink twice.

Hudson came up behind me and leaned down to wrap his arms about my waist, giving my soft stomach a squeeze. He loved it, and I loved him doing it. Made me feel good about myself that I had found a man who admired my thick thighs and tummy rolls. I felt… beautiful and adored.

"So, what are your plans today? It's Sunday and the weather is great, want to go for a walk or something?" he asked me and I turned my head to land a soft kiss on his lips. "Hang out at my place and go swimming?"

I nodded and tried to finish chewing my food, swallowing it down so I could answer. "Actually, that sounds great to be honest."

"I'm in!" Garth and Willow said in unison.

"Great, I'll pick up some food and drinks and we can have a barbecue."

"How about you head home and get things ready and I'll swing by in a few hours?" I suggested.

"Sure, or you can just come with me when I leave," he offered as he let go of me and went to stand beside Garth.

"I actually just want to run some errands and… get some things for Alyssa's wedding." God, I was bad at this lying thing.

"Actually, can you drop me off at home, Sav? I want to freshen up, get my bathing suit, and pop a few headache pills," Willow asked.

Thank you Willow! "Sure, I can."

"Okay, well I guess we have a plan. I'll call Flynn and Alyssa, see what they're up to. You coming with me, Garth?" Hudson questioned as he grabbed his keys from the top of the refrigerator.

"Yeah, sounds good. I'll help you set up," my roommate offered.

Hudson leaned down one last time and kissed the tip of my nose. "See you soon, beautiful."

"You sure will," I winked at him, and then waved at Garth. I hated that I just lied to the man I had fallen for, but if he knew what I was about to do, he would have tried to talk me out of it, or wanted to come with me. But I needed to do it on my own.

I texted Chris and asked him to meet me down by the mall in front of Gilby's Diner.

Here we go!

CHAPTER FOURTEEN

*S*avannah

WHILE WILLOW TOOK another small nap on the sofa, I got to work packing up all things Chris-related. Into a box went some shirts hanging in my closest, DVDs, and a few stuffed bears and trinkets he had brought me. Even the stupid hair comb I kept in my side drawer as a reminder he once shared my bed. As for the photos, I didn't think either one of us needed them as a reminder of times gone by. All they were to me were memories of happy times always mixed with heartbreak and a feeling of unworthiness. But now I knew better. I knew I was valued and treasured and that every inch of me, curves and all, was loved.

The moment Willow jumped into my car she knew something was going on, so I confessed where I was headed. "Are you mad!" she screamed so loud, my foot automatically hit the brake in the middle of a busy street. A car horn beeped behind me and I clutched at my chest.

"What the heck, Will! You almost caused me to crash." She turned in her seat to glare at me, and I waved a sorry out my window as I put my foot on the accelerator. I didn't want to look at my friend's super pissed face right then.

"Savannah, you can't go see him on your own. He's… he manipulates you every time."

I shook my head. "No. Not this time. I've fallen for someone else, and trust me, I'm not letting anyone jeopardize what I have with Hudson." Willow sat back in her seat. "I think I should come with you, just to be on the safe side."

"No, absolutely not. I know you just want to protect me, but I need to do this. I need to see him on my own and say goodbye once and for all." Pulling into Willow's driveway, I put the car in park and looked at her.

"I don't like this one bit, Sav, but… I guess I don't have a choice in the matter."

"Hey, I promise it's going to be over super quick. I'll hand him his box of things, say goodbye, and be back here before you know it to pick you up and take you to Hudson's, okay?"

Willow opened the car door and climbed out. She leaned down and pointed at me. "I'll be timing you."

I nodded. "Okay you do that. Give me half an hour,

that's it." With that she closed the car door and I reversed out of the driveway.

WHEN I PULLED up in front of the diner, Chris was already there seated at one of the outside benches. I reached into the backseat and grabbed the box containing his things and exited the car. When he spotted me walking towards him, he stood from his seat to greet me. As I took a seat, he leaned down to kiss my cheek, but I saw it coming and shoved the box between us. "Here you go, your things," I said as I pushed it into his arms.

He got the hint yet instead of returning to the long wooden bench on the opposite side of the table, he sat down beside me.

"Wow, you look beautiful today," he complimented and lifted a hand to catch the stray piece of hair that had fallen from my ponytail.

But I was faster and swatted his hand away to fix it myself. "I'm just wearing shorts and a tank, Chris."

He cleared his throat. "Still, you look beautiful. You always do."

I turned to face him, and got straight to the point. "Look, I don't know how to say this in a way that won't hurt you, but you need to stop calling me, texting me, and… well, just kind of disappear from my life Chris. It's ov—"

"I miss you." He cut me off and my mouth fell open.

Not in shock, but at the nerve of him interrupting. That's what he did. He always spoke over me, took the lead, and, once upon a time, I had let him. I was his enabler.

I went to yell at him about his rudeness, but something stopped me. The look in his eyes perhaps. The sadness that told me he really was missing me. He ran a hand through his thick black hair, that was usually styled without a tendril out of place.

"I'm so sorry, Sav. Jeez, I know I screwed up time and time again. I thought I wanted something else, to sow my wild oats or something, but seeing you a few weeks back in the bridal store made my heart ache. Heck, it almost leaped right out of my chest when my eyes landed on you. I know I was an idiot and I made the biggest mistake by letting you go."

I shook my head. "It's too late for that. I've fallen for someone else who wants me for me. I never felt like I measured up to the woman you dreamed of having. But here's the thing, I like myself, no, I love myself just as I am. Curves, stretch marks, cellulite, the works, and being with someone like you, who keeps searching for perfection... well, that's not me."

"No, you are perfect and I see that now," he pleaded.

I had the feeling I wasn't going to get through to him, so I cut my losses and stood up to leave. And he stood as well, throwing the box on the table. Before I knew what was happening, Chris had wrapped his arms around me and pressed his lips to mine. I knew I should have slapped his face the moment he did it, but… something felt different.

I wrapped my arms around his shoulders and deepened the kiss, closing my eyes and trying to focus on the moment. Nothing, not a damn thing stirred within me. No feelings of love nor emotion towards the man that had consumed me. The tears of loss I had cried over him ending it between us many times—there was nothing.

I paused, and broke contact with him, and placed my hands on his chest to gently push him away. I searched his eyes, as he searched mine. "You feel it too, right? The emptiness." I asked Chris and he nodded as he stepped out from the bench seat.

He reached for the box and tugged it under one arm. "Yeah, I felt… nothing." Six months ago that statement would have been like a slap to my face, only this time it was relief. "Wow, I guess this time it's really over, hey?" he stated.

I nodded and reached for his hand. He held mine for a moment, as we silently said goodbye to one another. "Yeah, it is."

CHAPTER FIFTEEN

$\mathcal{H}$udson

"Do you think we have everything we need?" Garth asked as he grabbed some of the shopping bags off the counter.

"Are you kidding! We have meat for you and Flynn, salads, beer and ice, ice cream, and more packs of potato chips than necessary. I'm pretty sure we have everything," I assured my friend as he followed me out of the food store and back to the truck.

Placing the groceries in the back tray, Garth still seemed unconvinced. "What about cheese?"

I looked over at him. "Why do we need cheese?"

He shrugged. "For dips or something, I've noticed Willow always goes for the dips when we're all together."

I climbed in behind the steering wheel shaking my head the entire time, a smile forming on my lips as Garth climbed up also into the passenger seat. "You really have it bad for her, hey?"

Garth rubbed at the back of his neck with one hand and turned the A/C on with his other. "Yeah, I got it bad, and it sucks too."

"Why's that?" I asked as the cool air began blowing.

"Because I've never felt this way before and that impossible woman doesn't feel the same. I want her to see me the way Alyssa and Sav look at you and Flynn." Garth turned his face away from me and glanced out the front window. "Speaking of Sav… isn't that her over there?"

I looked to where he was pointing and sure enough, there she was, sitting on one of the benches outside of Gilby's Diner. I smiled in adoration until I saw who she was sitting with.

"Ah, should we go over?" Garth questioned.

I watched her stand up from the seat, and just as quickly Chris stood. Right before my eyes, I watched as the bastard wrapped his arms around my girlfriend's waist and planted one right on her lips.

"Oh man…" Garth whispered and I could feel him looking at me, but my eyes stayed trained on the scene happening in front of my very eyes. I waited to see if Savannah would push him away and slap the crap out of him for touching another man's woman, but my heart broke the moment I watched her close her eyes and wrap her arms around his shoulders.

"Holy meatballs," Garth opened up the door and I knew he was seconds away from stopping whatever was happening outside the diner.

"Get back in, we're going," I growled and he halted.

"Dude.."

"I said get back in, Garth," I warned, my temper at an all-time high. He did as I said and climbed back in, shutting the door. I peeled out of the parking spot and headed for home.

I was fuming, unable to really comprehend what I had just witnessed. Garth pulled his phone from his shirt pocket. "Don't you dare message her or let her know we just saw that."

"Come on man, it's Savannah. Maybe what we saw wasn't what we saw, you know?"

"No, I don't know. I think we both saw what the heck just happened and my girlfriend let that asshole kiss her!" I yelled out my frustration and hit the steering wheel.

"So what are you going to do?"

"I don't know. But for now this conversation is over."

"There's got to be an explanation."

"She lied to me. She said she was grabbing things for the wedding."

"Well maybe she was and she ran into him," he came to her defense and it was wearing thin.

"No, she had a box of his stuff from what it looked like to me, which means she didn't just run into her ex, she planned it and then lied to me. So no more questions or defending, this conversation is really over."

Garth shut his lips the rest of the drive and for that I was grateful.

I thought about the missed calls I had seen from him on her phone. I tried to play it down like I wasn't worried, but I was fooling myself. I knew how hard it was getting over whatever they had. I was patient, but honestly, it broke me a little. Yet what if they had been seeing one another and I was the stupid fool unaware of what was happening? I thought she felt the same way I felt about her, but I was obviously wrong on that front, too.

"So… you going to cancel the pool party day?" Garth asked as I pulled into the driveway and turned off the engine.

"Nope," I told him as I climbed out.

"For some reason I don't think this is going to go so well."

Slamming the truck's door, I whispered under my breath, "Yeah, we'll see."

CHAPTER SIXTEEN

*S*avannah

IT FELT SO FREEING to finally say goodbye to my past, to the man who screwed me over time and time again. I wanted to place the blame solely on his shoulders, but truthfully, I enabled him. I allowed him to treat me with such disrespect. But not anymore, I had learned my lesson and in a way I guess I had my ex to thank for that.

Pulling out of the parking lot, I headed back to pick Willow up, and I couldn't wait to be around the people I loved, mostly Hudson. Yeah, I was head over heels in love with him and I wanted to be with him. I also wanted to find the perfect time, maybe at the end of the pool party, to say those three huge words to him. I did love him, and I couldn't imagine my life without the tall, handsome man that made my heart beat a little faster every time I thought about him.

I beeped the horn as I pulled into Willow's driveway, and ten seconds later she was walking towards me, wearing her swimsuit beneath an aqua kaftan she had on with sandals. And to top it all off, a can of scotch and cola in her right hand with a beach towel in the other.

She climbed on in and threw her towel into the back seat. "How'd it go?" she pulled her sunglasses down her nose and looked at me.

"It went well actually. Chris and I are done and dusted." She didn't seem at all convinced by my statement.

"And he knows that? Like really knows that he doesn't have a hope in hell of ever worming his way back in?"

"Yeah, he knows," I assured her.

She held her can up to me. "Well here's to moving on," she toasted before putting it to her lips.

I shook my head as I backed out of the driveway. "What happened to your party days being over?" I asked her.

"Yeah, that starts tomorrow." *I didn't believe a word of it!*

WE ROCKED up to the pool party and made our way round back. The moment we rounded the corner, my eyes landed on Alyssa, who was laying on one of the pool lounges in her black bikini, looking as if she was asleep. I loved her confidence. Even as a plus size girl, she had no issue wearing a two-piece and embracing her curves. And damn, did she rock it! Me, I wasn't quite ready for that step yet, so I still wore a one-piece with a small attached pink frilly skirt.

I flung my bag on the lounge beside her and sat on the edge. "Still suffering sweetie?" I spoke low.

"Kill me." She lifted her hand and pulled the shades down her nose to look at me with blood shot eyes. "Then why are you here and not at home sleeping it off?" I giggled at her, my hangover gone thanks to food in my stomach and a few more headache pills than recommended in my system. She pointed to the pool and I looked to see Flynn floating around in it. "He made me come because, apparently, that's my penance for having strippers when I enforced on him that he wasn't allowed."

"It wasn't her fault, Flynn!" I called out.

"Nope, it was all on me!" Willow yelled as she did a cannonball into the water right near his head. She dove out from under the water and wrapped her arms around Flynn's shoulders, and smacked a big sloppy kiss on his cheek. "Forgive me?"

He tried to look annoyed, and he probably was but before too long he was all grins as he dunked her under the water and then went below the surface. When they both popped back up, Will was sputtering but then he kissed Willow's cheek. "Okay, I forgive you. But next time let Garth know earlier, he could have arranged strippers for me too," he winked.

"That better have been a joke!" Alyssa called.

"It was," he winked, and then swam off.

I looked around. "Where's Hudson and Garth?" I asked.

Alyssa waved her hand towards the back entrance to the house. "Just getting the ice for the cooler and some snacks I think. Anyway, they'll be out in a moment."

I was happy with that, and decided to take off my dress and dive in for a quick swim. The beating sun was scorching my skin. Just a quick lap and then I would get out, dry off and have Hudson lather me up with sunscreen. I wasn't as bold as Willow by diving in; instead, I used the steps and adjusted to the water one step at a time. I got all the way up to step two when I had the onslaught of water from Willow and Flynn splashing at me, as I tried to stupidly block it. "You two are so immature," I barked out, not impressed with their behavior.

"Just get in already," Willow laughed as she waded towards me.

I stepped up one, but wasn't fast enough. Her hands grabbed hold of one of my arms and pulled me in. I popped my head out of the water and scowled as I pushed my hair out of my face.

"You're the meanest person I know Willow Sanders!"

She laughed as she swam backwards. "And yet, you still love me."

In that moment, I didn't, as my body adjusted to the water. But she was right, I loved her dearly, and underneath the tough exterior she was the sweetest most caring person I knew. Her heart was even bigger than Alyssa's. She also won brownie points because every day she set aside a caramel spiced cupcake with honey cream cheese frosting. Yeah, she knew the way to my heart all right.

Hudson and Garth exited the house, each carrying one side of the cooler. I waved when they both spotted me, but Garth gave me the saddest smile, and Hudson… well, he just looked away. I frowned, wondering what on earth was wrong.

Swimming to the edge of the pool closest to the table they placed the food on, I leaned against the side. "Hey, guys. Coming in for a dip soon?" I asked.

Hudson still didn't turn but Garth did. "Ah… maybe later Sav. We're… going to put some meat and potatoes on the barbeque. And, you know, salads and all. Busy, busy," he said, but there was something in his tone that had my alarm bells firing off.

I pulled myself out of the pool, a hard feat. When you're in water, you feel weightless, but trying to get this body out over the side instead of being smart by using the stairs was ridiculous, and I wound up having to roll myself over and up onto my knees.

"I'll help you guys, just give me a sec," I said as I ran to dry myself and place on my dress.

"I don't want your help," Hudson said louder than I expected and the splashing in the pool stopped.

I looked at Alyssa who was now sitting up as if on high alert. All I thought was, *Did he really just yell at me? He didn't want my help!* I finished placing on my dress and made my way around the pool to confront Hudson and whatever crawled up his butt today.

Garth looked as if he was trying to block my way, like he was Hudson's bodyguard or whatever else, I wasn't quite sure. He held his hands up. "Sav, maybe you just need to…"

"To what?" I folded my arms when he refused to move out of my path.

"Give Hudson a moment."

"A moment for what?" I asked confused, trying to look around the body that didn't look as if he was going to move.

"To, to… um, well, you see..."

I wasn't waiting for Garth to finish his sentence. I pushed him aside and skirted past. I grabbed Hudson by the arm and pulled him around to face me with all the strength I had.

What I came face to face with almost broke me.

$\mathcal{S}$avannah

HE PULLED free from my hold and marched away from me. "Hudson, wait!" I called as I ran after his speedily retreating steps.

He spun on me before he hit the back steps, looking down at me with hurt in his eyes. "Is there anything you want to tell me?" he spoke, his words slow, and I felt I had sunken an extra foot towards the ground as my face began to heat.

"I don't understand what you're asking me, Hudson. You're not making sense. No, I have nothing to tell you," I replied. Internally, I panicked because that wasn't true, but if I told him what had happened between me and Chris, he would take it all wrong.

"So that wasn't you I saw kissing your ex outside of

the diner?" he almost spat, his voice cracking as if holding back… grief.

I heard the gasp behind me from Alyssa, but I refused to turn. What I really wanted to do was keep my eyes locked with Hudson's but even that was impossible as I lowered my head.

"It's not what it looked like."

"Oh, I saw it with my own eyes and you didn't exactly pull away, Sav."

Trying to figure out exactly how to word my response, so he could see it meant nothing and before I finished coming up with the right thing to say, Hudson turned and walked away from me and into the house.

Taking a step ready to chase after him, Willow grabbed me by the arm and spun me around. "What the heck Sav,? What's Hudson talking about?" she shook her head just as confused as he had been.

"What's going on?" Alyssa came up to stand beside Willow, her face just as shocked as everyone else's. Garth and Flynn passed by us, my best friend's fiancé's steely eyes boring into me.

As soon as the guys were in the house and out of ear shot, I gripped my wet hair. "Oh God, it's a big misunderstanding. I kissed Chris and somehow Hudson was there to witness it all. Well, no, let me rephrase, I didn't kiss him, he kissed me, and I didn't exactly pull away as fast as I should have."

"Damn it, Sav, you told me you guys were over, that you were just dropping his stuff off!" Willow crossed her arms with irritation.

"Why didn't I know about any of this?" Alyssa stared at me sadly, as if I had purposely kept her out of the loop.

"Lyss, he kept calling and this morning I decided to give him the stuff I had been holding on to and end it all for good." I assured her before turning to Willow. "It is over, Will, and I'm glad he kissed me because it made me realize something—I'm not in love with him, like not at all."

I didn't want to stand there a moment longer, I needed to talk to Hudson. I turned and ran up the stairs only to be blocked again, except this time it was by Flynn. "Please move. I need to explain everything to him." He shook his head and stood imposingly in front of the sliding door.

"He's not in the state of mind to hear your excuses, Sav."

"Let her in Flynn Andrew Colson or I—"

"No," he cut Alyssa off.

From that moment all I knew was my actions had made a huge impact on everyone, as my best friend and her fiancé were arguing and yelling at one another. Willow placed her arm around my shoulders, as the tears began to fall and led me back down the stairs.

"Come on, let's give him time to calm down and you can try to call him later," she suggested as she grabbed my keys and led me around the side gate towards the car.

"I didn't mean to hurt him, Will, honest."

WILLOW DROPPED me off back at my house and insisted on staying, but in the end I begged her to leave and give me time to wrap my head around the huge kerfuffle I had caused. The moment she left, I fell onto my bed and just cried as I tried not once, not twice, but fifteen times to call Hudson in the hopes he would pick up. When that didn't happen, I sent him a text trying to explain what happened and to let him know it meant nothing. The last message simply read, *"Please give me the chance to explain, xx."*

Placing my phone on the bedside table, I rested my head on my pillow and stared at the damn thing just hoping the screen would light up with a reply or even a call. But after an hour, my eyes got sleepy and puffy from all the crying and closed themselves.

I heard the soft knock at my bedroom door, but didn't bother to even respond. The squeak of the hinges alerted me that someone wasn't waiting for to me answer, and then I heard Garth's voice. "Hey, just wanting to make sure you're okay," he said softly.

When I didn't even reply, knowing that he, too, was probably mad at me for the betrayal, Garth came and sat on the side of the bed and placed his hand on my arm.

"Wanna talk about it?" I covered my face with my hands to try to hide the fresh wave of tears that started falling. "Shuffle over," he said. He laid down on the bed beside me and wrapped his arms around me as I soaked the front of his shirt with my waterworks. "I just don't understand why, Sav. I've gotten to know you and it seems out of character."

I heard the love and confusion in his tone. I had grown to love him, too. He had become such an important friend in my life. "It didn't mean anything. I look back and know it was stupid, but it was also something I needed to do, and I don't know how to explain it."

"You hurt him, you know?" Garth whispered as he kissed my forehead.

"Yeah, I do know and I don't know how to make it better."

We never said another word and as Garth held me, somewhere in that time we had both fallen asleep. The thing that woke us was Hudson, standing beside my bed, angrier than he had been that afternoon. "Why do you keep hurting me, Savannah!"

The loudness of his statement jolted us both awake and Garth rolled off the bed hitting the floor with a loud thud. I sat up and, through puffy eyes, watched as Hudson stormed from the room. I hurried off the bed and took off after him, sleep muddled and frightened he was going to leave.

"Hudson, it's not what it looks like," I explained as I caught up to him as he swung the front door open, Garth now right beside me.

He spun on us and glared down at me. "Seems to be your only defense today. And you..." his eyes turned to his friend. Poor Garth didn't stand a chance as the fist went flying into his face. I screamed, as he was knocked into the side of the door with the force from the blow.

"What the heck man! I would never do anything with Savannah. We just fell asleep while talking, I didn't realize I cocked a leg on her hip. I think you broke my cheekbone," he groaned as he cradled his face.

"Good." That was Hudson's final word as he walked away from us and climbed into his truck. Garth ran back inside and I heard the jingle of his keychain. He stopped in the doorway. "I'm sorry, Sav. I have to make this right with him now before his imagination runs away with him and he reads even more into the situation." And just like that he peeled out of the driveway in pursuit of his friend.

While he ran after Hudson, there I was left standing in an even deeper hole, I had created, and I didn't know how to dig my way out of it.

CHAPTER EIGHTEEN

Hudson

TWO WEEKS! It had been two whole weeks since I had seen Savannah, and it was killing me. I didn't want to eat, sleep, work... heck, I didn't want to do anything except wait for the next text or call she would try to make. Two days ago that all stopped.

Maybe I had finally done it, and she had got the hint I didn't want to speak to her any longer. Sometimes I didn't because it hurt too much, other times I just wanted things to go back to the way they were before the kiss. I tried not to let her silence get to me, but there we were, at the rehearsal dinner at the river ranch and there was no Savannah to be seen. I thought I would bump into her once we had checked into the cabin we were all sharing for the weekend for my brother's wedding, but she never showed up.

Garth and I had made up after he pestered me for three hours straight by knocking on my front door. Had to give it to the guy, he wasn't leaving until he claimed his innocence. I believed him, and I could see how torn he was. He wanted to be there as my best friend, but he had also gotten really close to my girlfr… to Savannah.

As we sat down at the long dining table, I glanced at Alyssa and Willow across the table. Willow shot me daggers every time she caught me glancing her way and I couldn't understand why. It was not like I went out and kissed my ex. No, that was her friend that had done that, so why was I in her bad books all of a sudden?

I leaned over to Garth who was sitting next to me and whispered. "Where's Savannah?"

"She didn't want to step on your toes, so she decided to skip the rehearsal tonight. But she'll be here for the wedding tomorrow." I should have been happy with that, relieved even, but that was far from the case. *Was this how life was going to be now? She and I avoiding one another even though her friend and my brother were soon to be joined in marriage.*

After the dinner was over, the main wedding party made their way over to the small chapel on the expansive property and ran through the walk. My job was easy, as I just stood at the front behind my brother, pretending the rings were in my pocket. When Willow made her walk down the aisle carrying pretend flowers in her hands, she glared at me, and sneakily gave me the bird.

"Man she hates you today," Garth stage whispered.

"Ya think?" I replied sarcastically.

Teresa was there, giving Alyssa away. As they made their way down the aisle, I appreciated her mother's humor, as she waved her hand like the damn queen all the way to the front of the chapel. The whole thing felt wrong not having Sav there though.

And when the trial ceremony was over, I was supposed to escort my partner down the aisle and out of the church, yet there I was walking alone. No, it wasn't right and I had begun to question my own actions in the entire situation. Maybe I should have just heard her out. Maybe I should have answered her calls, at least tried to understand her a little bit. But my pride had gotten in the way.

When everyone returned from the chapel to have a night cap before we all retired for the night and got our beauty rest for the pending nuptials, I sat by the fountain outside the main building on the property. I heard gravel crunching beneath shoes and I turned my head to see my brother walking towards me with two beers in hand. He passed one to me and sat down on the fountain's edge to join me.

"Everything all right?" he asked.

"Yeah, this love stuff is hard though."

Flynn nodded as he took a sip of his drink. "It is, and there are going to be times when breaking points come. I'm not walking into marrying Alyssa blind, thinking every day is going to be perfect. But man, she's worth the hard times."

I rubbed at the back of neck in awe of my brother's confidence. "I should have listened to her," I admitted.

"I agree. Look, I was as pissed as you when I heard what she did, but Alyssa talked some sense into me." I looked at him with astonishment in my eyes "I mean, I don't condone what she did, but sometimes things happen and they may not be as big as we make them in our minds."

"So, should I call her now, or wait until tomorrow or even after the wedding?" Damn, I was so confused. A part of me wanted to hear her out, another part of me dreaded what I would hear. I was a friggin' mess.

Flynn placed his hand on my shoulder as he stood up to leave. "You'll see her tomorrow. Leave it until after the wedding… but no arguments on my wedding day because Alyssa will skin you alive if you ruin it for her."

"Noted," I raised my beer towards him.

However, that didn't mean I had any idea what I was walking into or how the atmosphere between us would go. The one thing I knew without doubt was I was looking forward to seeing her face tomorrow. I missed it.

CHAPTER NINETEEN

S avannah

THE WEDDING WASN'T until two o'clock, giving us time to have our hair and makeup done. I purposely didn't go the night before, wanting to give Hudson a moment to enjoy the place before my onslaught arrived. Yeah, I wasn't backing down in the slightest. He wanted to see how I felt about him, so that man was about to find out in a big way.

The moment I arrived at half past eight that morning, I dumped my bag into the cabin the wedding party would be sharing and went in search of him. Opening one door after another, I got frustrated when no one was in the place. I texted Willow.

Where are you all!

At the main house having breakfast. Sooo good!

Is Hudson there with you?

Nope, haven't seen him, but your very annoying roommate is. Weirdo keeps looking at me! Oh and have you met Flynn and Hudson's friend Andrew? Yummy!

I couldn't help but laugh a little. Willow and her man-zoning eyes. And she got those guys every time. She looked like an angel with her blond hair and sweet-looking ways. Ha! She was anything but on the inside. She told you how it was, and didn't take any crap from anyone. I think it was her way of protecting herself from ever being hurt.

Placing my phone on the kitchen counter of the cabin, I got to work on my plan. The amount of trips to my car was crazy! As I checked the time on the clock above the television, I realized I only had fifteen minutes left before I had to be at Alyssa's cabin for the day of prepping, so I had to rush.

"God, I can't believe it's my wedding day!" Alyssa spun around in front of the mirror, her cream-colored lacy, floor-length dress accentuating every beautiful curve on her body. "I just…"

"You look beautiful!" I said, trying to hold back the tears of happiness I felt as I stared at my best friend. She was radiant and I felt so blessed to be sharing the day with her.

"You look wonderful, sweetheart, but can you hold

still so I can place this veil underneath your bun?" her mother asked as she chased Alyssa around the room.

"Well, I for one am actually kind of glad you convinced us to wear these dresses. They've grown on me," Will added as she took a sip from her champagne glass. "Now, are we ready to get going? I can hear the music playing from here," she exaggerated, and Alyssa nodded as she placed a hand on her stomach; I could almost feel her nervous butterflies myself.

Walking to the small table by the cabin door, I picked up her bouquet and handed it to her. She smiled and then gave me a quick hug. "I'm so… oh boy I'm nervous and happy all rolled into one."

"Let's get you married!" I exclaimed as I opened up the door for her to exit.

The bridal party climbed into the white Rolls Royce that would drive us the mere two minutes to the small white chapel that sat right by the lake on the edge of the property. The scenery was so beautiful, but all I could think about was Hudson, and my own nerves rose to the surface. I hadn't seen him in two weeks, and my eyes missed his face. My body longed for his to be against mine, and my lips pined for his to touch mine once again.

As the usher opened the door, Willow was the first to enter and start her walk. I took a deep breath and on cue I began my slow steady steps down the aisle towards the front where Flynn waited for his bride to enter. He looked as cool and collected as always, and just as dashing in his suit and perfectly styled dark hair, like a model from a popular magazine.

My eyes moved to the man next to him and my lips quivered. *Hudson.* He was so handsome, and all I wanted to do was drop my small bouquet of roses and run into his arms. But he didn't even glance my way as his eyes were trained on his brother's back. It broke my heart, as I reached the front and took my place. As the music changed again and I turned to watch Alyssa enter, I looked at Garth. He mouthed, "Beautiful" to me and I thought about. how sweet he was by knowing exactly what I needed.

The nuptials were short and sweet, and I spent the entire time trying not to cry from the sentiment in the small chapel as vows were exchanged and commitments made. I glanced over at Hudson more times that I cared to admit, but still he never looked at me once.

"I now pronounce you husband and wife," the celebrant announced. Before he even had time to give permission to kiss the bride, Flynn had Alyssa bent backwards and was causing quite the cheer from all that attended.

I clapped in happiness, along with everyone else as they linked hands and began their walk down the aisle as Mr. and Mrs. Colson. I stepped forward and Hudson held out his arm for me to take. But still, he said nothing as I looped one arm through his. As we smiled and greeted the guests, I leaned into him. "Are you going to say anything to me today?" Nothing, not a damn word!

The day was turning into a nightmare and I just had to bide my time as we got through the photo session, which seemed to last forever, before we made it to the reception. As soon as we made our entrance, Hudson once again let go of my arm after escorting me to the table and then disappearing.

"Jeez, he's being such an ass today," Willow exclaimed as she handed me a flute of champagne as we walked over to the large windows that looked out onto the lake.

I threw it back swiftly, needing the alcohol to help dull my senses. "Yeah."

"That's all you have to say?" her mouth fell open. "I'd slap that disrespect off his face. He could have at least played nice for one day. Like at his brother's wedding!"

I shrugged and grabbed another champagne from the waiter that wandered by and cradled it to my chest. "Maybe he doesn't want to give me false hope. You know?" I really hoped with everything I had that he would. I needed him to know how sorry I was, how my heart longed for a second chance at the best thing that had ever happened to me.

"Where is that gorgeous man?" Will changed the topic as her eyes began searching the room.

"What gorgeous man? Garth?"

She laughed. "Heck no, not Garth. Flynn's friend Andrew. Oh my, didn't you see him at the chapel? Fifth row from the front, groom's side."

I shook my head at her. Only person I was looking at

was Hudson. "You need to focus on Garth, he's your partner for the day, so be nice to him."

"Yeah, yeah I will. He's just… I mean he's sexy and all, but he also infuriates me, like big time!"

I laughed as I took a sip of my drink. "I'm so telling him you called him sexy."

She pointed at me. "Don't you dare. His ego doesn't need the boost."

My eyes zoned in on Hudson on the other side of the dance floor. It looked as if he was heading to the bathroom. I quickly passed my glass to Willow. "I'll be back in a minute," I told her right before I took off and wove my way through the guests already on the dance floor.

As I rounded the corner, adamant I was just going to barge into the men's room and demand he speak to me, I ran into a brick wall. Well, figuratively. I actually ran into a tall male form. I stepped back and looked. "I'm so sorry."

"I'm not," he smiled down, and I actually blushed. I had never seen him before, but he was handsome in that country boy kind of way. Cowboy boots, dark jeans with a belt buckle, navy blue button-up shirt, and a smile that demanded you attention paired with deep sapphire eyes.

"I'm Andrew," he held out his hand towards me.

So *that* was Andrew, and Willow was right, he *was* handsome. "Nice to meet you, Andrew. I'm Savannah," I shook his hand.

"I know who you are, and I'm afraid to tell you that

I have been told to block your attempts at reaching Hudson."

I placed my hands on my hips. "Is that so?"

"It is. But my advice to you is if you really love him, don't give up that easily." He shucked me softly on the chin. "You seem like a sweetheart."

I smiled at him with a glint in my eye. "Thank you for the... pep talk. Don't you worry, I have a plan B in case he wasn't going to hear me out. "

"Well, I look forward to witnessing it."

As I turned to walk away, I couldn't help but look at Andrew one last time. I could see why Willow found him charming, and I had a feeling that wasn't the last time I was going to see him. But for now, I couldn't think about whether he was going to become an acquaintance; I needed to put plan B into action.

CHAPTER TWENTY

Savannah

IT WAS time for the wedding speeches and Hudson stood up first. I smiled along on cue, but I heard nothing that was coming out of his mouth, my stomach in knots at what I was about to do. I had literally zoned out, and had no idea it was even my turn until Willow nudged me.

Standing up, I held out my arm behind the couple and Hudson passed me the microphone. Clearing my throat I began. "I have dreamed of this day for my friend for many years. In my mind, it wasn't even half as beautiful as what the day has been, and to witness the love between Alyssa and Flynn is awe-inspiring." I knew I should have gone on and made it all about the new couple, but I hijacked the speech and just hoped they would forgive me for it later. "Yeah, I'm in awe of what I see, and I, too, feel that way about someone, right here in this room. Hudson," I turned to look at him, "I love you. I love you so much I can't breathe when I think about how much I hurt you these past few weeks. And if this is the only way you're going to listen to me, then in front of all these guests, I'm going to confess it all."

He stood up to leave, but before he could Flynn and Garth both placed their hands on his shoulders and pushed him back onto his seat. I would thank them both for that later. I turned to Willow and nodded, and just like that she took her cue and reached under the white banquet tablecloth and came back up with a big pink box. She stood up and walked to where Hudson was and placed it down in front of him as I continued.

"I love you so much, I made you a cake. I made it with love, for the man that I love." Willow flipped the top open so Hudson could see what I had done. "I wouldn't recommend eating it, and in case you can't quite tell those are my attempt at piped daisies on top of piped green frosting to represent grass. I always put daisies in your dead grandma's posies, which you were really buying for yourself. And so... we all lie sometimes, cause you did. But that's not the point! I love you and I'm sorry... like I'm really sorry and I'm confessing my lo..."

"Sav, stop," he laughed and stood from his seat. I lowered the microphone and just waited. I may have had a Plan B, but the speech was as far as I had gotten when it came to the reception. Hudson approached me, and gently pulled me back from the table, resting his hands on my upper arms. "Say it again," he whispered.

"I love you, Hudson." He shook his head.

"Now you say it," I replied. He closed his eyes, as if contemplating if he should. "I'm going to keep rambling on till you say it," I warned him. "I'm so sorry, baby. I never meant to hurt you, and I can see how much I have, but I promise it meant nothing. God, I know you don't believe that, but I don't regret doing it. Crap, even that sounds bad. But you have to believe me, I love you and only you. You're my every—"

Before I knew it, he bent me over backwards and his lips crashed into mine. Wrapping my arms round his shoulders, I deepened it as my mind screamed, *Home!* He was my home now, my world and I didn't want to be anywhere else, with anyone else.

"Okay everyone, ah, while they do that let's go cut the cake… the real cake, not the one Sav made that looks like a pig rolled around in mud," Garth announced over the clapping and the cheering that was erupting around us. Quickly following his statement came a loud, "Ouch!" I'm guessing Willow might have hit him upside the head for his comment.

When it came time for the wedded couple's first dance, Alyssa and Flynn glided across the floor like they were dancing among the clouds. But the second song had us all joining in and Hudson led me to the dance floor where he pulled me in close. I couldn't stop stealing small kisses every chance I got and my man didn't seem to mind in the slightest.

"Missed you so much," he mumbled as he kissed my neck, and I sighed in happiness. When he pulled back to look at me, I swore I fell more in love with him.

"I missed you more. I was so scared I had lost you. You're my everything, Hudson." And then I remembered. I stopped dancing, and reached for Hudson's hand, pulling him along behind me. "I need to show you something," I told him as I led him out of the reception hall and towards our cabin.

"Someone *definitely* missed me," he teased.

I looked back at him. "Oh, I missed you and believe me, you and I are catching up on... well later," I winked. Opening the cabin door, we entered and I continued to pull him towards his bedroom door. "Close your eyes and just stand here, but give me two minutes," I instructed.

When he did so, I walked into his room and made sure everything was ready. "Okay, you can open them," I said as I grabbed his hand and pulled him in. When he opened his eyes, he laughed in delight as he surveyed the room that was lit with a few candles and an even bigger surprise.

"You must have brought every snow globe in Seattle!"

I grabbed one from the bedside table and shook it before passing it to him. "You're not wrong. I went to every souvenir shop I could find. I know they're not as good at your mother's were, and I know they're not from travelling the world, but..."

"They're perfect." Hudson stepped towards me and wrapped his arms around me.

"I also made you a bracelet, it's under your pillow.

"You did?" he asked as he kissed his way down to my neck.

"Yep, it's a be-my-boyfriend-again bracelet."

"Well, I'll wear it with pride," he said.

And that was it, I was head over heels, pinch myself in love happy. I knew we would still need to talk, but in that moment, we were so done with the talking.

EPILOGUE

G arth

DAMN IT! Everything was turning to crap. I was at my best friend's wedding, celebrating this momentous day in his life and all I could do was watch the woman of my dreams flirting with that stupid lady charmer Andrew!

To be fair, he wasn't a bad guy, but my girl game definitely got easier after he left two years ago to help on his family's ranch in Texas. Turned out we have similar taste in women, and competition was something that came naturally to us. So, watching him on the dance floor with Willow was more than I could handle.

To top it off, my other best friend and my roommate had disappeared from the reception altogether and Sav wasn't answering her damn phone! I needed back up, I needed encouragement, yet there I was sitting by the bar, watching the woman I adored grinding herself against my new nemesis. I needed to come up with a plan and fast because I wasn't about to just sit by and watch her fall into the arms of another man. I needed a game plan!

Get ready to fall in love with Willow & Garth's story in
book three of The Curvy Lane series,
PREORDER YOURS NOW

ABOUT THE AUTHOR

So this is me in short. I'm plus size and completely adorable (or so my husbands tells me) A momma of three princes who light my world. I drink way too much coffee, chocolate is a staple. I love to write after midnight and my passion for short stories will never fade. With such a limited amount of time to enjoy quiet writing, I have mastered the skills of fitting a lot into a small amount of pages. Humour keeps me smiling and well.. if you've read my books you'll know that I put a lot of myself into the characters. And to answer your questions. My best friends and I forgot the part about growing up and love every minute of it.

This is going to be an epic journey and one I hope you come along for! Join my street team and have some fun! or just drop by and say hello…

Love to all xo.

Come say hi!

www.sarahgai.com

ALSO BY...

Thank you so much for reading Ready to Bloom by Sarah Gai.

If you liked this, than I hope you continue to read my books and get ready to fall in love with book Three, Bit of Spice! Also if you have a moment, please leave a review from the place you purchased. They mean the world to an Author xx

Chick Lit

The Curvies

Curve My Song (Book 1)

Curve My Attitude (Book 2)

Curve My Heart (Book 3)

Curve My Valentine (Book 4)

Curve My Treasure (Book 5)

Romantic Comedy

Sparkles in Love (Book 1)

Amber in Love (Book 2)

May & Sam (Book 2.5) *Bonus with Amber in Love!*

Lily in Love (Book3)

Haley & Damon (Book 3.5) *Bonus with Lily in Love!*

<u>Nelson Brothers</u>

    Jaxon (Book 1)

    Kayden (Book 2)

    Andrew (Book 3)

    Bailey (Book 4)

<u>Curvy Lane Series Coming</u>

    Just as Sweet

    Ready to Bloom

    Bit of Spice- June 2020